Dragon's Web

Book 1 of the Pipe Woman's Legacy

Lynne Cantwell

hearth/myth

a hearth/myth book

Table of Contents

Chapter 1

This whole thing is my mother's fault.

Of course, Mom would blame White Buffalo Calf Pipe Woman for picking her – Naomi freaking Witherspoon – to be the facilitator/vessel/face of the Gods' New World. And then she'd blame my father for knocking her up.

Dad would blame Grandfather, if he could bring himself to blame anyone. Really, if you ask me, Dad got the best of the whole deal – he got Mom, who he'd wanted forever, and he got the kind of acceptance, and even reverence, that most skinwalkers can only dream of. But if it hadn't been for Grandfather's vision, none of this would have happened.

Grandfather himself would go all Ute shaman on you and say that human concepts don't apply when the gods are involved. "There is no one to blame, granddaughter," he would say. And has said it to me. More than once.

Grandpa Drew, who's a Lakota Wolf Dreamer, would just laugh.

And my baby brother Webb would simply look at you with that infuriating, ageless gaze of his and tell you that none of it matters. Blame doesn't matter, and neither does fate. Everything happens the way it's supposed to, he'd say, no matter what we do. There's no room for chaos theory in Webb's world. It's all tied together: yank on a string here, and your action will have a predictable result there. Looking for the cause is a waste of time. The important thing is the result.

Feel free to ask him whether that means our destinies are immutable. Go ahead – ask him. I have, countless times, in varying degrees of desperation. I guarantee you won't get a useful response. He'll only smile enigmatically and go back to whatever monstrosity of an art project he happened to be working on when you opened your mouth.

Gods, but it pisses me off when he does that. It's easy for him to be all mystical. He's not Sage Wakinyan Curtis, miracle offspring of Joseph and Naomi Witherspoon Curtis and/or White Buffalo Calf Pipe Woman and Coyote. He's not the one who has been destined from birth to save the world.

Mom says she understands my frustration, but I don't really think she does. After that little white buffalo calf bowed to her, her mother shielded her from most of the attention the world would have bestowed on her. And anyway, Mom was twelve – almost a teenager – when it happened. I've been living with this thing – this stupid prophecy, or curse, or *geas* – my whole life.

I suppose I should be fair and say that Mom and Dad have done their best to shield Webb and me from the worst of the craziness. They didn't exactly put a moat around the family homestead, or even an electrified fence. But we grew up pretty isolated in our mountain conclave, for all that we're only a few minutes from Denver. There were plenty of times when the faithful tried to set up camp outside our gate, or in the national forest land that adjoins our acreage in the back. Typically, Dad would handle it – shapeshifters have a talent for figuring out how best to scare people off – but there were a couple of times when Mom had to call the police or the Forest Service to get rid of them.

And it's been getting worse as our neighborhood has become less isolated. Mom and Dad say that when they first moved here, there were only a few houses nearby, and none within about a mile of us. But it's built up since then. And we're getting more squatters in the National Forest, thanks in large part to the Earth's increasingly inhospitable environment. Sea levels have begun to rise, so people who used to live near the ocean – those who can afford to, anyway – have been migrating to higher ground. At the same time, temperatures in the Northern Hemisphere have been rising a little bit every year, making the deserts even more difficult to live in than they have historically been, and the Great Plains are threatening to turn into another Dust Bowl. Sure, the optimal climate for farming has shifted farther north, but it's not like farmers can just homestead there, the way America was settled back in the pioneer days. It's more than just Native Americans living in their way now. And the current residents don't really have anywhere to go, because north of them, where the permafrost is starting to melt, is a vast sea of mud.

So the Rocky Mountains have had quite the influx of new residents, and that's taxing our natural resources. Water, in particular, has always been a scarce commodity in a historically semi-arid area like ours. It's gotten worse lately, though. A lot worse. And surprisingly fast.

My parents' friends, Charlie and Winnie Frank, own a ranch on the other side of the Continental Divide in Rifle. They drove over for a weekend just before I left for my junior year of college, and one of the recurring topics of conversation during their visit was just how dry it had gotten.

"We're having to buy water almost every week now," Charlie told my dad at dinner on our patio. "The creek's down to a trickle when there's any water in it at all."

My parents exchanged an uneasy glance. I didn't need to be a mind-reader to know what that was about – the creek on our property was bone-dry, too. "Well," Dad said, "it's pretty late in the year."

Charlie shook his head. "Not that late. And it's usually a gusher in the spring, what with the runoff from the melting snowpack at higher elevations. That just didn't happen this year."

"We got a decent snowfall," Winnie said, helping herself to more baked beans. "But somehow it didn't come down the mountain to us."

"I wonder where it went," Mom said, frowning.

"Sage will fix it," said Dad. He must have caught sight of my expression, because he added hastily, "After all, that's what she's going to college for. Right, honey?"

"Right," I said, making an effort to calm my temper. "That's the theory, anyway." It was supposed to be a science pun – *theory, get it?* – but Mom and Charlie are lawyers, and so it kind of went over their heads. Dad gave me a weak grin; he runs a construction company and so he's kind of a numbers guy, despite his supernatural side. Winnie gave me a kind smile and went back to eating. Webb acted as if he hadn't even heard me.

Dad's comment wasn't that far off the mark. I'm majoring in environmental engineering at the University of Colorado in Boulder, and doubling up on some requirements so I can get my bachelor's and master's degrees at the same time. I want to solve the problem of climate change so humanity can keep living comfortably on this planet. Environmental Studies would have been an easier route, but it's too theoretical for me – too many *what ifs*. Too many options. No, I'm a numbers girl. Hard-and-fast facts are all I want to deal in. Just one right solution for every problem. Even if it's not so easy to figure it out.

Grandfather spoke up then. "Sage *will* fix it," he said, echoing Dad, but the way he said it made it sound like a prophecy. Then he smiled at me in benediction, his head nodding just a bit, as it had recently begun to do.

I felt my face grow warm under the kind regard of everyone at the table. To cover it, I ducked my head and stood. "I need to talk to Kerry and firm up our plans for tomorrow." I shot everyone a tight smile. "Thanks for dinner, Mom. It was great." And I turned and fled.

In all likelihood, Grandfather meant his comment to be encouraging. He'd been expecting great things from me ever since I was a baby. They all had.

"What a thing to pin on a kid, you know?" I said to Kerry via Skype. I had called her as soon as I'd reached the sanctuary of my bedroom.

Her 3-D holographic image, seated on a holographic chair that appeared to be about three feet from me, issued a long-suffering sigh. She'd been hearing this refrain from me ever since we were kids. "You know what Aunt Shannon would say, don't you?" she said.

I rolled my eyes. Of course, I knew what her aunt Shannon would say – she was Mom's best friend. "She'd say I need to get over myself."

"And she'd be right," said Kerry. "Are you packed yet?"

I glanced around my bedroom. Books in a crate, check. Clothes in suitcases, check. Unlike a lot of college kids, I didn't have to haul everything back and forth with me; during the school year, Kerry and I lived in a formerly-trashed house that my parents had bought for a song during my freshman year of college. Dad and his best friend, who Webb and I called Uncle George, had spent a few months renovating it into habitability again, and then Kerry and I had moved in. She started out majoring in comparative religions, but then she switched to psychology. She claimed the programs weren't all that different since the gods' return, and psychology paid better.

There were days when I wanted to be Kerry Hanrahan – and not just because she wasn't marked for sainthood. She was adorably petite, with a turned-up nose, flashing green eyes, and these dark blond ringlets that swished around her head when she moved. Sometimes I felt like a galumphing mess next to her. I had inherited my father's build – tall and skinny, which looked better on him than on me – and my mother's arrow-straight black hair. My face isn't bad,

I guess, but I still can't seem to get any dates. I'm fairly intelligent – *Sage Curtis, girl engineer!* – which puts a lot of guys off. And then there's the legendary family thing.

I tell you what: being tall, smart, and infamous brings *all* the boys to the yard.

The house in Boulder had three bedrooms, and in the past, Kerry and I had had another roommate. But our roomie for the previous two years had graduated, so we were going to have to find someone else this year.

I turned back to Kerry. "I think I'm good to go. I just need to throw in the last-minute stuff in the morning, and then hit the road. What time are you planning to leave?"

"Probably around two," she said. She lived in Westminster, which was closer to campus than my house. "That should give me enough time to unpack before dinner."

"Works for me," I said. Then I sighed. "I should probably go back out and make nice with everybody. Charlie and Winnie are still here, and I don't want to be rude to them. I'll see you tomorrow."

"See you at the house," Kerry said with a grin, as her image disappeared.

I closed Skype on my tablet and went back outside.

The barbecue was breaking up. Charlie and Winnie, too, planned to hit the road in the morning. They were spending the night in the tiny cabin where we'd lived when I was born. The Franks wished me a good school year as I gave them both a hug.

Mom was stacking plates as Dad scraped down the grill. Webb had disappeared – probably off creating another of his fiber-art pieces, which he made from bits of yarn or fabric combined with found objects in unusual ways. His room was a fairyland full of his creations. When he wasn't annoying me, I had to admit that some of them were kind of cool.

"Sage, why don't you help Grandfather back to his place?" Dad said without turning around. I recognized that tone of voice; it wasn't a suggestion.

I looked at the old man – he's actually my great-grandfather – and sighed. "Sure," I said, bowing to the inevitable, and went to give him a hand up out of his seat.

"I'm not an invalid yet," he said, flashing an irritated look at both Dad and me. Dad shot what Mom always calls his Coyote grin over his shoulder, and I sighed again.

"Come on," I said. "Clearly he wants to get rid of both of us."

Grandfather grunted involuntarily as he creaked upright, and together we made our way down the path to his yurt, which sits up against the trees about 300 yards from the house. You might think it cruel that my parents make a ninety-plus-year-old man sleep in what amounts to a platform tent, but it's Grandfather's choice. The yurt, with its indoor toilet and its proximity to our place, is almost more civilized than he's comfortable with. At least Mom and Dad had managed to convince him to give up his wickiup.

As we crossed the bridge over our creek, I looked down with concern at the damp sand below. "Charlie's right about the water," I said. "It shouldn't be this low."

Grandfather nodded. "I know," he said.

When we got inside the yurt, he set about making tea while I straightened up a little for him. It didn't take long – most of what he owns is for ceremonies, and I wasn't allowed to touch it anyway. But I would always putter around a little bit in the kitchen, putting away his cooking utensils and positioning the plates and cups so he could reach them easily. "Who's going to do this for you when I'm gone?" I said, half-joking.

"Naomi is still pretty handy," he said, carrying the full mugs carefully as he shuffled to the table. "Sit, granddaughter. Drink your tea."

I folded myself into one of his homemade straight-backed chairs and took a tentative sip. "It's hot," I said, and put my mug back down.

He chuckled. "The first time I made tea for you, you were three years old," he said. "You took a big gulp, spit it out, and howled until it thundered."

I smiled thinly. I'd heard the story so many times that it was almost as if I remembered the incident. Which I didn't. But it was plausible; until I got old enough to master my emotions, my tantrums had often ended in thunder and lightning.

Just another reason why it's so great to be me.

He sobered, and regarded me kindly. "This will be a big year for you, Sage. You will face a major challenge, and how you meet it will define the course of your life for many years."

I blinked. That *did* feel like a prophecy. "Did Blood Clot Boy tell you that?" I said lightly, testing my mug of tea with another careful sip.

He laughed. "Ah, Sage. How you gladden my heart." He shook his head, still smiling, and took a long slurp from his own mug. "No," he said, "Blood Clot Boy is not involved in this message. I've heard it from other spirits – the wind and the water."

"Water?" I perked up. "Did the water spirits tell you where the snowmelt went, and why it's been so dry?"

"The climate is changing," he said.

"Not like this." I shook my head. "Not this fast. Something else is going on." I gazed out his kitchen window for a moment, and then brought my focus back to him. "Is this part of the challenge I'll face this year?"

"The spirits weren't specific," he said.

"They never are," I said ruefully.

"Often, they are not," he corrected me gently. "But if I had to guess, I would say there is a reason this problem is being brought to your attention now."

I gave him a dubious look. "You mean Charlie and Winnie came here for a reason? Come on, Grandfather. You know how I feel about that stuff."

He shook his head at me. "You will have to acknowledge your birthright sooner or later, granddaughter," he said. "The sooner you do, the more time you will have to learn how to wield it, and the more effective you will be when the time comes."

I couldn't look at him. Instead, I tilted my head back and closed my eyes. "I know," I said. "I know. I just wish I could get rid of it." I looked straight at him, then. "Sometimes I wish my mother hadn't ever met the goddess."

He covered my hand with one of his. "I know the feeling," he confessed. White Buffalo Calf Pipe Woman had turned *his* life inside out, too.

I took his hand and squeezed it gently. His fingers were dry, but his grip was strong. "Are you okay out here?" I asked. "Sure you don't want to move into my room while I'm at school? You're welcome to. You know that." He began to shake his head even as I went on, "Mom and Dad would be so much happier if you came inside. They'd worry less about you."

"Thank you," he said. "I prefer it here." He looked around and sighed. "And some days, even canvas is too confining for me."

"Uncle George thinks you're crazy," I said with a grin.

He smiled back. "Which of us do you think is more sane?"

I conceded the point. Uncle George was pretty crazy. I finished my tea and got up. "Thanks for the tea, Grandfather. Will you be all right?"

He waved me off. "I will be fine. You go on. Make us all proud of you this year."

"I'll do my best," I said as I gave him a hug.

As I reached the door, he called my name. I turned to look over my shoulder at him. "Don't forget that you can fly," he said.

"How could I?" I said, wincing. "Good night, Grandfather." And I shut the door behind me.

Like I said, I'd been able to call thunder – albeit inadvertently – since I was a baby. And I figured out how to shoot fire from my eyes when I was six or seven. Which surprised not only me, but also the bullies who were hassling Webb for knitting on the school playground. But I didn't start flying 'til after I hit puberty.

I was thirteen the first time it happened. I was just beginning to get the hang of the tampons-and-pads thing, and coming to terms with what it all meant. And then I started having odd dreams – dreams in which I seemed to lift out of my bed and soar away, above our house, along the Front Range of the Rockies, and over the city of Denver.

The dreams exhilarated me. I had such freedom when I flew! I felt no pressure to excel, no responsibility to save anyone. All I knew was the wind in my face, the air currents supporting my wings, and the sense of liberation as I burned a trail across the sky.

Yes, *burned*. I guess I forgot to mention that I'm allied with Thunderbird. My mother is half Lakota. The Lakota believe that Thunder Beings live in the west, that lightning shoots from their eyes, and that their wings create the wind as they fly across the sky, bringing rain clouds in their wake. They're friendly spirits, usually, believe it or not. But it's a really bad idea to piss them off.

Anyway, one night, I woke up from one of these dreams in my sleep t-shirt, straddling a pine branch about a hundred feet above the ground. "Dad!" I shrieked, clutching the trunk tightly. "Help!" In my terror, I'd managed to call the thunder. The wind had risen to meet it, and my perch was swaying. "Dad!" I screamed again.

It seemed like an eternity before he arrived as an owl. He stayed with me through the whole rescue operation. Uncle George brought an extension ladder, and Mom brought Dad some clothes so he could shift back into his human form.

I burst into tears when I set foot on solid ground again. "Make it stop!" I wailed, clinging to my father, who was supposed to know about this stuff. "Make it stop!"

The next day, we all huddled with Grandfather and Aunt Shannon. I explained to them about my dreams, and Grandfather explained about spirit travel.

"And you've always awakened in bed," Mom said. "Right?"

I nodded. "Until last night." I turned to my father. "How could I have gotten up into that tree?"

He shrugged. "You flew."

"But...."

He went on to explain that when he heard my cries, he and Mom went to check on me and discovered the patio door wide open. They figured I had sleepwalked out, then transformed and taken wing while still asleep.

By this time, I was shaking. "But how do I keep it from happening again?"

Dad was grinning from ear to ear. "Why would you want to? Flying is great!" Shapeshifting, I knew, was his release valve. When things got too complicated for him, he'd shift into his coyote form and hunt prairie dogs or rabbits. When he needed a wide view, he'd take to the skies. Now he had a daughter who could fly, and I realized with a sinking feeling that he was imagining all sorts of high-altitude father-daughter bonding sessions.

"You don't get it, Dad," I said.

His face fell. "What don't I get? Didn't you think it was fun?"

"It was great 'til I *woke up in a tree*," I said. And then I burst into tears.

Dad looked like I'd struck him.

As Mom wrapped me in a hug, I moaned, "I don't want to be weird. I don't want to live in a weird family and I don't want to have to save the world. I just want to be normal."

"Every teenager wants to be normal," Aunt Shannon said, putting a hand on my shoulder. She meant to comfort me, but I was too upset for it. I struggled free of both her and Mom and ran to the doorway. I could feel the sparks gathering behind my eyes as I turned to face them all.

"But I'm not 'every teenager,' am I?" I cried. "I'll *never* be normal. I'll always have laser eyes and I'll never be able to just get angry. And now I'll have to police my dreams. I'll have to tie myself to the bed every night, so I don't wake up in a *tree* again." Tears were spilling down my cheeks; I swiped at them as thunder rumbled outside, punctuating my desperation. "Sometimes I wish I'd never been born!" And I turned and fled, out of the house and up into the mountains, as the skies opened above me.

For once, my parents didn't come after me. I think they didn't know what to say.

The rain gradually died away, as did my tears. I was drenched and starting to shiver, but I didn't care. I hoped fiercely that I'd get sick and die, because that would solve everything.

I was kind of a mess that day.

It was Webb who finally showed up. He came bopping up the trail as if nothing had happened. "Hey, Sage," he called.

"Go away," I croaked. I'd sobbed and screamed until I had no voice left.

"I made you something," he said, and held it out to me. "Go on. Take it. It's your favorite color and everything."

It looked like a tangle of orange yarn, crumpled in his hand. I took it and stretched it out until it took the shape of a sort of net bag. "What is it?" I asked him suspiciously.

"It's a dream helmet," he said confidently. "If you put it on before you go to sleep, it will keep your dreams inside your head. Then you won't wake up in a tree again." He took it back from me. "Here, I'll show you." He slipped it over my head and tucked the strap under my chin. "There. How does it feel?"

"Like you just wrapped my head in yarn," I complained. "I bet I look like an idiot."

"So what else is new?" he said with a mischievous grin.

The thing was, it *did* make my head feel more secure. And I knew my little brother had a way with yarn; just a few years before this, he had knitted a bag for capturing Lucifer's essence, and it had worked. So if he said this assemblage of orange yarn would keep my dreams grounded, I was inclined to believe him.

I wore it to bed that night, and every night thereafter. And I never woke up in a tree again. But I also never learned to manage my ability to fly, and I had no idea how badly that would bite me in the ass later on.

The little brother speaks.

Gods, sometimes Sage is *so* unfair. I didn't have to make her that dream helmet, you know.

And I don't know where she gets off, calling me inscrutable or whatever it was. It's not my fault that I know the future, any more than it's her fault that when she gets mad enough, we get a localized sound-and-light show.

Here's the thing: I am *heyoka* to Sage's Thunderbird. I was born backwards – a breech baby – and I've been doing odd things ever since. Take the knitting. One day, I found a baby blanket that Mom had started knitting years before. Mom is not the artsy-craftsy type, and she'd given up on it after just a few rows. Anyway, I pulled it out of the bag and just instinctively knew what to do. No YouTube videos, no nothing. I just started knitting. I was three years old at the time. You could say it caused a bit of a sensation.

Mom and Dad thought I'd grow out of it when I started school, but as Sage said, I didn't, and the other boys gave me a hard time over it. There was one time in first grade when I came home in tears because a third grader had ripped my project out of my hands and flushed it down the toilet. Grandpa Drew and Grandma happened to be visiting us at the time, and Grandpa Drew took me for a walk.

Grandpa Drew knows quite a bit about being the odd guy. He began having Wolf dreams when he lived in Indiana, far from anyone who could help him make sense of them, and it got him into trouble in Vietnam. He ignored a message from one of his dreams, and because of that, he was wounded during the fall of Saigon. They had to amputate his left arm just below the elbow. It messed him up mentally for quite a while.

Anyway, he took me for this walk, and told me about that – as much as a six-year-old could understand, anyway – and then he told me his theory. "Webster," he said – I'm named after him, but nobody ever calls me Andrew except my teachers – "Webster, you are going to have a hard row to hoe in this life. A *heyoka* always does."

"What's a *heyoka*?"

"It's a sacred clown." And he went on to explain that if a Lakota dreams about a thunderbird, he is inducted into the society of these sacred clowns. The good news is that a *heyoka* can speak truth to power by using satire. The bad news is that they have to do everything backwards.

"You mean I have to walk like this?" I asked, turning around and walking backwards.

He laughed. "Not always. But you're likely to know a lot of things before Sage does. Before anybody does."

"I already do," I said. I'd been having dreams or visions of the future that seemed to come true, and I had been too scared to tell anyone – even Grandfather. I was afraid people would laugh at me, like they did for my knitting. But now I told Grandpa Drew about the dreams, and he didn't laugh. On the contrary, he told me to be very careful about sharing what I learned.

"Knowing the future is like living backwards, in a way," he said. "But it comes with great responsibility. Not everyone wants to know the future. Not everyone *needs* to know it. And some people should *never* know it. You're going to have to be smart about what you share with who." He shook his head. Then he brightened. "But hey, you get to give your sister hell whenever you think she needs it. So it's not all bad."

That sounded like a fair trade at the time.

As it's turned out, there are some things I never learn about until it's too late. Anything that I have a hand in? Can't tell you how it will turn out. So I have no idea whether, say, Kerry and I will ever go out.

Not that I'm interested in her or anything.

Let's   move   on.

Chapter 2

Traffic in Boulder was a nightmare, of course, particularly around the university. I'd expected it, given that all the students were coming back to town, but it didn't mean I was happy about it.

Well, okay. I was cranky that day for a number of reasons. I hadn't slept well after my chat with Grandfather. I kept mulling over what sort of unwelcome challenge I might face this year.

And when my brain got tired of circling that track, it would go off-road for a while and ponder where all the snowmelt had gone. I kept weighing and rejecting possibilities. Streams were nature's drainage system; the runoff from the melting snow should have ended up there. Even if it soaked into the ground really fast, it would still percolate through the soil and between layers of rock, and end up in a river eventually. That's the way a drainage system works.

Unless the drainage system was stopped up somehow. Or unless the snow was evaporating before it had a chance to melt and drain away – but then, in theory, the excess moisture would fall as rain. And that hadn't happened, either.

Some kind of underground catchment, maybe? Or some sort of meteorological anomaly that was sucking up moisture here and dropping it elsewhere?

I hadn't been paying a lot of attention to weather anomalies over the summer. Despite my association with Thunderbird – or more likely because I wanted to avoid it – meteorology wasn't really my thing. I was more interested, as I've said, in the engineering aspects of climate change: not *why* or *how* it's happening, but how to fix it so it doesn't happen again.

One of the best things about the gods' return was the number of arguments They settled. Yes, we have free will; no, nobody who lives a good life will be shut out of Heaven, whatever you perceive Heaven to be; yes, you have to treat everybody the way you'd treat yourself, even if their skin is a different color and even if you don't like their gods; and no, climate change is not some kind of liberal plot to force humanity back into the Stone Age.

Moreover, there wasn't much the gods could do to stop Earth's climate from changing. Earth is a closed system; the planet has only so much fossil fuel, only so much clean water, only so much breathable air. The gods did what they could to mitigate the damage, but the only way They could increase supplies of the good stuff would be to wipe out the whole planet and start over – which, unsurprisingly, nobody was in favor of.

Maybe if the gods had come back sooner.... But no, it wouldn't have helped. We'd have still had morons who insisted on wasting time arguing with Them.

Anyway, the point is that even though we'd pretty much converted to renewable fuels and cleaned up our manufacturing processes as much as possible, the climate was still changing. And it would continue to do so for another hundred years, minimum. Things were definitely going to get worse. The only way we could make it better would be to roll back the damage by finding a way to extract carbon dioxide and other greenhouse gases from the air and put them safely back into the ground.

Which was why environmental engineering appealed to me. If I could be one of the people who figured out a solution to this puzzle, I'd be fulfilling my destiny – I'd be saving the world! – and I wouldn't have to use any of my superpowers to do it.

So in a way, I was grateful to Charlie and Winnie for giving me this puzzle to work on. I just wish it hadn't kept me awake the night before I had to drive back to college.

By the time I turned onto University Heights Avenue and pulled into the driveway, I was ready to get inside and go to bed. Unfortunately, I still had to unpack the car. And Mom had sent along a cooler full of leftovers from the barbecue, which had to be unloaded and stowed right away.

I was pulling the last duffel bag full of sweaters out of my car when Kerry pulled up. I dropped the bag on the concrete and sagged against the door to shut it, as she leapt from her car. Clearly, she'd had more sleep than I had. "I'm done," I called. "Just let me put this inside and I'll move my car to the street."

"Take your time," she said. "I don't have time to unpack right now, anyway. I need to go meet a prospective roommate." She grinned.

I stared at her. "You found someone already? That was fast."

"I'm just that good," she said airily as she grabbed a tote bag from her passenger seat. "No, actually, I ran into Gemmie last week, and she told me this friend of hers was looking for a place. Says she's really nice. Very quiet. So I called her on my way up here just now." She stopped in front of me, eyes narrowed. "You look like hell."

"Thanks a lot," I said. "I couldn't sleep last night. Who's the prospect? Anyone I know?"

"I don't think so." She shouldered my duffel and headed up to our front door. "Hilary Something-Asian."

That rang a bell. "Takahashi?" I asked, following her into the living room. At her nod, I said, "I do know who she is. She was in my intro computer course freshman year. Really smart. I think she ended up majoring in computer science."

Kerry sighed dramatically. "Another brain trust," she said. "I guess I'll just be the dumb one."

I socked her playfully on the shoulder. "Cut it out. You're plenty smart."

"Not like you." She tossed her head, looking for all the world like Epona, the Celtic horse goddess with whom she was allied. "I'll just have to settle for being part of the horsey set."

"Neigh," I said, and she socked me back.

I blame my exhaustion for what happened next.

An hour or so into unpacking, I couldn't keep my eyes open any longer. I'd thrown in my dream helmet at the last minute (yes, I still wore the thing every time I went to sleep) but I couldn't remember which cranny I'd stuffed it into, and I didn't want to try to stay awake long enough to tear through all my bags to find it. So I set the alarm on my phone for twenty minutes, and stretched out on my bed.

My last conscious thought was, *What can go wrong in twenty minutes?*

I flew over beautiful but unfamiliar territory. A vast plain spread out below me, glowing green and gold in the late summer sunshine. Rapidly, I approached snowcapped mountains, higher even than the Rockies. I heard water trickling below me; it seemed to come from under the snow, and it occurred to me that if I followed the sound, I might find out what had happened to our snowpack. I banked and cruised lower, leaving a trail of smoke in my wake, looking all the while for the source of the sound.

I was just about to land when I heard a low chuckle. "There You are, Perun," a sibilant voice said in a language that I was sure I shouldn't have been able to understand. "I've been waiting for You."

Perun? Who the hell is Perun?

"Time to end this," the voice said. And out from behind a snowy rock face shot the grinning head of a dragon.

In my surprise, I floundered in the air and nearly plummeted to the ground. "Who are you?" I cried.

At the sound of my voice, he drew back in confusion. "Who are you?*"*

"I asked you first," I said.

Childish sarcasm was probably not my best strategy. "Whoever you are, little firebird," he sneered, "you will rue the day that you interfered with My plans." He opened his mouth – to breathe fire, I suppose – but I beat im to it. I focused my fiery gaze on his gaping maw and let 'er rip. He screamed as his tongue sizzled. Then, with a roar, He launched himself into the air at me.

I sat up abruptly, my heart pounding, and snatched up my phone. I had another five minutes before the alarm was set to go off, but I wasn't about to chance sleeping again without the damn helmet. Instead, I fired up the phone's browser and looked up *Perun* and *dragon*.

What I found left me more puzzled than ever. How did Veles, the Slavic god of the underworld, come to be in my head?

I closed the browser and called home.

"Miss us already?" Mom teased as she answered her cell phone.

"Totally," I said. "Always. Hey, Mom? We don't have any Russians in our family tree, do we?"

She paused. "Not that I know of," she hedged, always the lawyer. "Although given my track record in that regard, nothing would surprise me any more." I grinned at the joke. Mom hadn't known she was half-Lakota until she was well into her thirties. "Why do you want to know?"

I told her about my dream. "I'm pretty sure the language the dragon was speaking was Russian," I finished. "Or something Slavic, anyway."

"But you could understand him."

"Yeah. But it was a dream."

"I *hope* it was a dream." She sounded worried. "Let me give Kurt Lange a call."

"What good will that do?"

"His people are closer to the Russians than ours are," she said. "I'll call you right back."

I shook my head as the phone went dead in my ear. Because my family regularly consorts with the gods, I knew that Mr. Lange, the

CEO of H&M Hrafn International, was also Thor, the Norse thunder god. What I'd seen online seemed to indicate that this Perun fellow was the Slavic Thor, more or less. But that didn't mean Mr. Lange would know Perun, and it also didn't mean that he'd have any insight into why Veles had wanted to attack Him. And by extension, me.

I pulled the scrunchie out of my hair and redid my ponytail a little more neatly. Then I got up. Mom's *I'll call you right back* sometimes took a while. I might as well get a little more unpacking done while I waited.

In the meantime, Kerry returned with Hilary in tow. She hadn't changed over the past two years: she was still self-effacing, with fluttery movements that belied her nervousness. She had a slight, almost wispy build. She wore her dark hair in a bob with bangs down to her eyebrows, and wire-rimmed glasses with tiny lenses perched on her nose. In short, she looked like a stereotypical Japanese student, like you'd see in some manga. All she needed was a demure pleated skirt to complete the look.

And then she opened her mouth. "Y'all are so kind to offer to let me stay here," she said in her Carolina accent. *Kind* came out as *kahnd*, almost, and *here* sounded more like *heah*.

"You're helping us out, too," Kerry said. "C'mon, let me show you the room." They moved on down the hall as Kerry continued her realtor pitch. "You'd have the smallest bedroom, but it's right next to the back door and the laundry room. So if you were out late studying or something, you could slip in and out of the back door and not bother us as much."

"That sounds fine," said Hilary. Her *fine* sounded like *fahn* to me. "I do keep odd hours from time to time." *Tahm tuh tahm.*

I needed to quit doing that if she was going to live here. Although given enough time, I figured I'd get used to her accent. Eventually.

I plastered a pleasant expression on my face as they emerged from the vacant room. Hilary was all smiles. "This is perfect. I'll take it." *Ah'll.*

Cut it out, smartass brain!

"Great!" Kerry said, and we all shook hands. "Let me get the rental agreement for you to sign, and your key." She disappeared into the kitchen. I could hear her rooting through the drawers, looking for the spare key.

"So," I said brightly, turning to our new roomie. "You're a computer science major, right?"

She shook her head. "Statistics. But we run a lot of simulations, so there's a fair amount of programming involved. You're in ENVS, correct?"

It was my turn to shake my head. "Nope. Too squishy for me. I'm in EVEN."

"Squishy?" she asked, frowning.

"Too many variables," I said. "Engineering problems have just one right answer."

"She doesn't do well with options," Kerry said with a grin. She held out a key to Hilary. "Here you go. Move in any time. Where's your stuff right now?"

"Storage," she said, a little too quickly. "It's in storage. In Louisville. I, um, need to go get it. And close out the account. I should go do that now." She ended with a little giggle, one hand to the base of her throat.

Kerry looked at her with a speculative glint in her eye. "How much are you paying for that unit?" she asked. "Because I've got some stuff that I'd love to get out of my room, and there's no place else to put it here."

I knew exactly what she was talking about. She had scored an elliptical trainer from the trash behind a frat house last winter. "I told you to take that thing home at the end of the school year," I said. "But did you listen to me?"

"I thought I'd use it to get in shape," she said. "Then I got too busy. Anyway, how much is the rent on your unit? I can just pay it for you."

Hilary had a frantic look about her. "Oh no, you can't. I mean, I've already told them I'm leaving."

"I thought you said you still had to close out the account," I said.

"I do," she said, wide-eyed. "But I emailed them to tell them I'm leaving. I think they've already rented it to someone else."

"Guess you'll have to get your own storage unit," I told Kerry as she shot me a cranky look. "You should've just taken the thing home."

"Anyway," Hilary said, stepping around us, "I'll be back later. Thanks again!" She waved and walked out the door.

As the front door closed, Kerry raised an eyebrow at me. "How likely would it be, do you think, that a storage unit would turn over that fast at the *start* of a school year in this town?"

I nodded thoughtfully. "Good point. What are you saying? You think we just made a mistake?"

"I'm not sure," she said, her eyes on the door. "But I guess we're gonna find out."

Chapter 3

Mom called me later that night to say that she had left a message with Mr. Lange. She texted me the next day to say she was still waiting to hear back. *If he doesn't contact me today, I'll call him again,* she promised.

There was no word from him on day three, either. Mom was pretty upset about it, but I was inclined to let it go. I was still half convinced he wouldn't know anything useful. And besides, I found my dream helmet shoved into the bottom of my purse and went back to wearing it, so – presto! – no further nocturnal contacts with Veles. And anyway, classes had started and my life was getting busy.

Hilary moved her stuff into her room that first night, while Kerry and I were at dinner. It turned out that she hadn't been kidding about her wacky hours. We hardly ever saw her. Kerry joked that it was almost like rooming with a ghost.

"I don't care, as long as she pays her rent on time," I said.

"And doesn't haunt us," she added. "Although I guess she can't, if we never see her."

I had been looking forward to starting Water Chemistry ever since the barbecue with Charlie and Winnie. The professor, Dr. Raymond, had seemed like an approachable guy when I'd had him for a class the previous year. I figured that if I was going to get to the bottom of the mystery of the missing snowmelt, talking to him would be a good place to start.

The gods made sure my first class was memorable. I overslept, and spilled coffee on the shirt I'd intended to wear, and couldn't find another shirt that went with my slacks. By the time I rushed into the classroom, I was ten minutes late, and Dr. Raymond had already begun his lecture.

Way to impress the prof you need help from. I crept down the steps of the lecture hall to the first available desk on the aisle. It was one of the those flimsy tubular steel numbers from the 1970s, and when I tried to stuff my backpack under the seat, one of the shoulder straps caught on the chair back and pulled the whole thing over.

My face flamed as the class erupted in laughter. Dr. Raymond regarded me with a bemused smile. "Everything all right, Sage?"

Of course he remembers me. Everybody remembers Sage the Savior. "Sorry, Dr. Raymond," I said as I tried to pull the desk upright. Just as I realized that my stupid backpack strap was still stuck over the seat back, throwing the whole thing off-balance, the guy at the next desk reached a long arm across and swept it off. "Thanks," I muttered in his general direction, and finally righted the desk.

As I slid into my seat at last, the guy held out my pack to me, the top loop hanging from one nonchalant finger. I restrained myself from snatching at it. Instead, I took hold and looked him in the eye.

Oh my gods, he was gorgeous. His raven-black hair dipped perilously close to one eye and swept back from there to hang in a short ponytail at the nape of his neck. His nose was hooked slightly, his chin had a dimple, and his brown eyes glittered.

"Thanks again," I said, trying not to stammer.

"Anything for Earth's Savior," he said with a slow shrug.

I shut my eyes so I wouldn't hurl a laser beam at him by mistake.

"May I proceed?" Dr. Raymond called with a smile.

"Yes! Of course!" I said as I fumbled my tablet out of my treacherous pack. Then I spent the next thirty-five minutes trying to stuff my self-consciousness and focus on the lecture. I swear I only glanced over at Gorgeous Guy two or three times.

Despite the delay at the start of class due to my splendiferous entrance, Dr. Raymond finished early and let us go. Briefly, I debated the wisdom of speaking to Mr. Gorgeous again vs. the likelihood that anything would come of it. But something prompted me to swallow my self-doubt. I turned to Mr. Hunk and stuck out my hand. "Thanks again," I said. "I'm Sage Curtis."

"I know," he said with a smirk. But he shook my hand.

"And you are…?" I prompted.

"Nobody," he said, still grinning. And still holding my hand.

I was certain I'd never seen him before, although his grin looked familiar. I pressed on, going for gentle humor. "And did your parents give you a name, or does everybody just call you Nobody?"

"Rafe," he said. "Rafe Orloff. I'm a transfer student."

"From…?"

"Alaska. Anchorage, to be more precise."

"Really? I've never been to Alaska," I said, "but I've always wanted to go. What's it like?" I knew I was yammering, but I couldn't seem to stop myself.

"Cold and dark," he said. "Everybody lives in igloos. And it snows all the time, even in the summer." His grin widened as he spoke.

I knew he was full of shit. But his comment helped me place where I'd seen that grin before: on my father. The cogs in my brain whirred and spit the conclusion out of my mouth before I could stop it. "Trickster," I blurted. "Probably Raven."

He dropped my hand in surprise. "You're good," he said.

"I get a lot of practice at home," I said, while my brain continued to chug away. "Did you say your last name was Orloff? You're not Russian, by any chance, are you?"

His mouth fell open.

"We need to talk," I said.

We grabbed drinks at Celestial Seasonings – tea for him, high-test coffee for me – and compared life stories. Although he pretty much knew mine already, so he did most of the talking.

"Dad is a bunch of stuff, but mostly Russian," he said. "Mom's people are Tlingit, from the Raven clan."

"Figures," I said. "Can you shift?"

"That's a pretty personal question from someone I've just met," he said in mock indignation.

I propped my chin on my hand and waited.

Finally, he sighed. "Yeah. But not like your father can. All I've got is bird and human."

"That's plenty," I assured him, and he seemed to relax a bit.

"So," he said, playing with his paper cup, "can *you* fly?"

The question startled me. "I…uh…it's complicated," I said.

"I've got nothing but time," he said, slouching back with one hand still wrapped around his cup. "My next class doesn't start 'til two."

Yeah, well, I don't want to go there right now. "What I really wanted to talk to you about was the Slavic pantheon."

"You changed the subject," he said gleefully.

"Yes, I did," I said. "What do you know about Perun and Veles?"

He shook his head, still grinning. "Woman's got a thing with Thunderbird, but she doesn't want to talk about flying," he said. "Wonder what *that* means? I bet it means she can't fly."

"Can we just talk about Veles for a minute?" I asked, on the edge of exasperation. "I had a dream about Him that wasn't exactly pleasant, and I'm trying to get to the bottom of it."

He dropped the snark. "You dreamed about Veles? How did you know it was Him?"

"I didn't at the time. I looked Him up online when I woke up."

"What did He look like?"

"Giant dragon." I shuddered at the memory. "Thought I was Perun. Got mad when He realized I wasn't. He would have burned me to a crisp, except I burned Him first." I pointed to my eyes.

"You killed Veles?" he asked in surprise.

"Gods, no. I just singed His tongue a little."

He nodded, his brow corrugated. "Good. It's too early in the year for Him to die. Where was this?" he asked.

"I didn't recognize the landscape," I said, making a mental note to ask him later about the significance of the time of year. "Tall, snowcapped mountains, but it wasn't here in Colorado. Don't ask me how I know that for sure. I just do."

"I believe you." His frown deepened. "Was there a tree nearby?"

I thought back. "No. There were, like, scrubby tundra plants. But nothing tall like a pine tree."

"Or an oak?"

"Definitely no oaks." I shook my head.

"And you were in the mountains when you met Him?"

"Yeah."

"How'd you get up there?"

I sighed deeply. "I flew, okay?"

"Ha!" he said, triumphant.

"But I only fly in dreams," I went on. "I've only *really* flown once, and I swore I'd never do it again."

"You didn't like *flying?*" It was as if I'd said I didn't like breathing. "How could you not like *flying?*"

"You and my father would get along just fine," I said, stifling a glare. "So what do you think the dream means?"

He sat back again. "I dunno. I'm going to have to think about it. Look into some stuff. I'll let you know what I find out."

As vague as that all sounded, I was grateful. "I'd appreciate it. So," I said, changing the subject again, "are you in EVEN?"

"Nope. ENVS."

I stared at him. "You're an environmental studies major? Then how'd you get into Water Chemistry?"

His grin came back at once. "I'm a Trickster, remember?"

The long answer was a little more complicated. He had transferred schools in part because of a climate-change-related research project he intended to complete either this year or next. Dr. Raymond was tops in the country in one facet of his project, and it had been his idea that Rafe enroll in this class.

"In other words," I said, "you sweet-talked the prof into letting you in." I knocked back the rest of my coffee to cover my smile.

"I think the official phrase is, 'By permission of the instructor,'" he said, rather loftily.

"Uh-huh."

"Anyhow, I've had all the prerequisites," he said. "And besides, word on the street is that you're some kind of savant at this stuff. With you helping me, I can't lose." He looked at me over the rim of his cup, eyes dancing.

I felt my jaw sag. We'd been getting along so well – even having a normal conversation about what my mother calls the woo-woo stuff – that I'd begun to nurture a hope that he was interested in me. My face, I mean, or my sparkling personality. But no. Of course not. Whatever made me think that Mr. Gorgeous Alaskan could be interested in *me?*

Disappointment made my tone overly sharp, even to my own ears. "And now you're sweet-talking *me*. I'm supposed to just roll over and hand you my notes – is that it?"

He shrugged. "Can't blame a guy for trying."

I'd just bitched him out and he hadn't noticed? That was it. I was done. I glanced at my phone and stood. "I'd love to continue this fascinating conversation, but I've got another class in ten minutes." Slinging my backpack over my shoulder, I said tersely, "See you Wednesday."

"I'll save you a seat," he called after me.

Like I'd sit next to you again, ever. I nearly turned and went back to bitch him out again, but I didn't want to be late for two classes in the same day.

Later that afternoon, I dragged my ass back to the house. I had finished one reading assignment between classes, although it had been tough to focus on my work. My brain kept going back to a vision of my backpack held aloft by one finger of an upturned hand – and the guy that hand was attached to.

I shook my head as I stuck my key in the lock. The guy was a jerk. And I had a ton of homework to do. I couldn't afford the distraction.

"Door's open," a muffled male voice called from inside.

Ah, shit. No way. I pushed my way through the door. Sure enough, Webb was ensconced on the sofa. One of his hands held the remote; the other was busily transferring some kind of vile chips from a plastic bag to his mouth. His enormous, smelly sneakers sat in a heap next to the coffee table.

I grabbed the remote and clicked off the TV. "And you're here why?"

"Nice to see you, too." He held up the bag. "Want a chip?"

I dropped my backpack and waited.

He lowered the bag with a sigh. "The art department had a field trip to see the mixed-media exhibit at the art museum," he said. "So I caught a ride. Dad's going to pick me up on his way home. He's working on a house in Loveland this week."

My eyebrows shot to my hairline. "*Dad* is picking you up? How did you manage to talk him into that?" Our father had a more-or-less strict rule against driving with other people in the car.

He shrugged. "I left it to the last minute, so he didn't have a choice. Can I have the remote back?"

"No. I have a lot of homework to do, and I need to be able to concentrate."

But he seemed to have lost interest. Glancing around, he asked, "So what time does Kerry get home?"

"Ah," I said. "Now it all comes clear."

Webb had had a thing for Kerry ever since we were little. He was forever tagging along with us, trying to interest us in his latest yarny thing. It drove me crazy, of course, but Kerry was always nice to him. I guess it didn't bother her as much because she didn't have to live with him. Anyway, it got so that he would basically attach himself to her whenever she was over. Which was a lot. And when he hit puberty, his adoration of her turned into – not an obsession, exactly, but I wouldn't call it just a crush, either.

For her part, Kerry just kept being nice to him. It's not that she encouraged him – she didn't – but she enjoyed any and all male attention. Even from a guy who was three years younger, who she thought of as her little brother.

The thing was, while Webb knew the future, the gods had given him a blind spot where his own future was concerned. So he couldn't see the train wreck coming. All I could do was advise him to find a girl his own age, and hope that he did it before he got his heart broken.

"You need to get over her, little brother," I said now. Again.

He shot me a disgruntled look and headed into the kitchen. "Got anything to eat? I'm starving."

"How could you be hungry? You were just eating chips," I said as I followed him.

"I'm a growing boy," he said as he ducked his head into the fridge.

"No, you're an annoying pain in the ass. What time is Dad supposed to be here? Please tell me it's soon."

He had reached into the fridge and was moving stuff around. "How come you have so many cucumbers?"

"What are you talking about?" I pushed him aside. Sure enough, the vegetable bins were full of cukes. "Wow." I gave him a mystified look. "They're not mine, and I don't think they're Kerry's. Hilary must have bought them."

"Who's Hilary?"

"New roommate." I looked again. "Jeez. That's, what, three dozen cucumbers?"

"Is she on some kind of cucumber diet?" he asked. "Some weird girly beauty regimen, maybe?"

I shook my head. "No idea. She's hardly ever here."

Kerry breezed in the front door. "Hi, Sage. Jeez, what a day. My profs didn't waste any time handing out homework." Then she caught sight of us standing in front of the open fridge. "Oh. Hi, Webb. I didn't know you were coming today."

"Neither did I." I shot him a glare, but he didn't even notice – his gaze was all for Kerry. I turned back to her, mentally washing my hands of him. "You didn't buy all these cucumbers, did you?"

"Nope, wasn't me," she said. "I noticed them this morning. They must be Hilary's."

"Wonder what she needs them for," I said, closing the fridge door at last. "I hope she plans to finish them before they turn to sludge."

Dad arrived around 6:30 and took the three of us out for pizza. We grabbed an L-shaped booth. Kerry and I slid onto the bench seats while Dad and Webb took the chairs facing us. After we'd placed our order, my father glanced around and shook his head. "This place hasn't changed a bit."

"I didn't think you went to CU, Uncle Joseph," Kerry said.

"I didn't. But George and I used to come here after we'd been up at Grandfather's place. That was before I met your mother, of course," he said to Webb and me.

Grandfather's wickiup had been near Boulder. Dad had taken us there a couple of times when we were kids. The wickiup was gone by then, and so was the sweat lodge that he'd used for his business. But there was still a great view of the plains, and a trail that led up to a beautiful meadow that Grandfather said was sacred to the Utes. Webb told me later that the spirits that had been there years ago had moved on. He made me promise not to tell the old man, but I think he knew.

"So you guys were cruising for girls, then?" I said, wiggling my eyebrows.

"Well, not here, specifically," he said. "But yeah, we'd hit the bars. I'd play foosball and George would try to score." He gave me his Coyote grin. "Hey, Webster, how about a game before the food gets here?" He laid one hand on Webb's shoulder.

Webb started. He'd been staring at Kerry, of course. "What? Oh, yeah. Sure." He got up and headed off with Dad.

I was about to advise Kerry for the *n*th time to have a talk with Webb when a hand grabbed my brother's chair and spun it around. "Fancy meeting you here," said Rafe, draping himself over the chair backward.

I rolled my eyes, even as my stomach lurched. Mr. Gorgeous Alaskan was the last person I wanted to see right now. Still, there was no reason to make a scene in the restaurant. Not until he started acting like a jerk again, anyway. "Kerry," I said, "this is Rafe. He's in my Water Chem class. Rafe, this is my roommate Kerry."

"Nice to meet you." He nodded at her. "Mind if I join you? Have you guys ordered yet?"

"Actually, we have," I said quickly. "And you're sitting in my father's chair."

"Oh," he said, and sprang up – nearly colliding with Webb, who was already coming back. "Sorry. I didn't mean to intrude."

"Not a problem," said my father, who was right behind Webb. "Foosball table was busy." He stuck out a hand in Rafe's direction. "Hi, I'm Joseph Curtis."

Guys would usually freak out when they came face-to-face with my father. Besides the standard *oh my gods I'm meeting her dad* nervousness, there was the tasty layer of *oh my gods and he's on a first-name basis with Jehovah* on top. But I had to give Rafe credit – if he was stunned to be caught usurping the chair of the famous Joseph Curtis, he covered it surprisingly well. Gamely, he shook hands with my father while I did the introductions. Dad invited him to stay – "With the amount of food we ordered, you'll be doing us a favor" – and told me to scoot over despite Rafe's, and my, protestations.

Rafe could have been a younger version of my father. It's not that they looked all that much alike – Dad's skin was a darker brown, like mine, and his hair was salt-and-pepper to Rafe's black. But they were clearly brothers under the skin. They had the same lively spark about them, as if each was poised to drop their veneer of civilization at a moment's notice and let chaos take over.

As I scooted over, I caught Webb looking at me, a speculative gleam in his eye. I knew that look. It usually meant he'd just had some insight into the future that I wasn't going to like at all.

I mouthed the word *no* at him. The last thing I needed in my life was more chaos. Even if it was a gorgeous hunk of chaos who wasn't flummoxed by my family.

His response was a fair imitation of Dad's Coyote grin, which did nothing to make me feel better.

Of course, the whole shapeshifter thing came up at dinner, because why wouldn't it? Doesn't everyone discuss the various animal forms they can mold their bodies into while stuffing themselves full of pepperoni and melted cheese?

"You know, Sage, I talked to Grandfather after you left," Dad said. "Raven could be useful."

"For what?" I asked incredulously.

"Flying," said Rafe, with a lopsided grin.

I closed my eyes before I fried them both.

"How about those Buffs?" Kerry said brightly, and the conversation turned to football. But I couldn't bring myself to contribute much. Dad's mention of Grandfather had reminded me of that damned prophecy. It was first down, in a game I had no interest in playing, and I was about to be handed the ball – whether I wanted to run the play or not.

Chapter 4

I had the best of intentions – honest, I did – but it was well into September before I got around to talking to Dr. Raymond.

The main snag was that Rafe and I had gotten into the habit of sitting next to one another in class, and then going for coffee – well, in his case, tea – right afterward. I know it sounds weird, given that I'd been so sure he was a jerk. But he hadn't renewed his request for my notes, and I was beginning to think maybe I'd overreacted that first day. Maybe he'd been joking, and I took it wrong.

So anyway, he kept asking and I kept going along. And it took me a few weeks to realize that I was using it as an excuse to avoid the momentous thing Grandfather had predicted.

When I figured that out, I realized I had to just do it. Even if it meant avoiding Rafe.

So on that day, I waited outside the room until Rafe had gone in. Then I entered the room and, without glancing his way, took a seat several rows ahead of him. I swear I could feel him staring at the back of my head all through the lecture.

At the end of class, I left my tablet on my desk and fought against the tide of departing students to reach the professor's lab table at the front of the room. "I need to talk to you about something," was my highly specific opening gambit.

"My office hours are listed in the syllabus," he said briskly as he slid his materials into his briefcase. Then he paused and said, in an incredulous tone, "You're not having trouble with the long-term project, are you?"

I shook my head. The long-term project was stupid easy, in my estimation. I had already finished the first segment, which wasn't due for another two weeks. "This is about something else."

He cocked his head.

"The lack of rain," I elaborated. "And what happened to last year's snowpack."

"Ah," he said, and stared at the back wall for a moment. "Can you come by my office Thursday at two? I'd like for Rafe to be in on the discussion, if it's all right with you. It may have a bearing on a project he's working on."

I stopped myself from rolling my eyes. There'd been no good reason for my subterfuge, after all. Of *course* Rafe would have to be involved, because that's the way things always worked in my world. "Sure. Although I may have to leave early. I have a class across campus at three."

"That's fine. See you then." He finished packing up and strode past me, up the lecture hall steps and toward the back door. He stopped briefly to say something to Rafe, who was still shoving his stuff into his own backpack. Rafe shot me a sideways glance and nodded, and then Dr. Raymond continued up the steps and out the door.

I dithered next to the lab table while Rafe fussed overly long with his pack. It dawned on me that he didn't intend to leave without talking to me, and anyway I was going to have to pass his desk to get out of the room. I kicked myself mentally for not sitting on the other side of the lecture hall, and went up the stairs to get my things.

"Still have time for coffee?" he called as I approached my desk.

"Sure." I scooped up my tablet and backpack and headed up to him. "Um, listen. About...."

He waved me off as he stood. "No worries. It can wait 'til we meet with Martin on Thursday."

That made me pause. "You're on a first-name basis with Dr. Raymond?"

He lifted one shoulder, but his cheeks were turning pink. "You could say he's a family friend. He went to college with my brother."

This was the first I'd heard of Rafe having any siblings. "You have a brother?" As I spoke, my brain ran on without me. Dr. Raymond was probably in his forties. "He must be a lot older than you, if he went to school with Dr. Raymond."

"My father was married before. Are you ready?"

I finished stowing my tablet and slung the backpack over one shoulder. "I am now."

He gestured grandly, a lock of hair falling adorably over one eye. I couldn't help but grin as I preceded him out of the room.

I was, as I've said before, no beauty queen, and that plus my IQ plus my weird family usually equaled zero dates for Sage. Or maybe one, and then the guy would run away really fast. So Rafe's attention had kind of blindsided me. I appreciated it, don't get me wrong, but I kept trying to figure out what his interest was.

It might have been as innocent as a feeling on his part that he'd found his tribe. Relationships with specific gods were more common since the Second Coming, but shapeshifters were pretty rare and usually still viewed with suspicion. He and my father had definitely hit it off, but Rafe hadn't peppered me with questions about him since then. So I didn't think that was it.

It had also occurred to me that Rafe might be one of those people who thought his own star would rise by associating with me. My parents had run into several of those over the years, so I thought I knew what to look for – and Rafe didn't seem to be that type.

We'd had a few celebrity stalkers, too. Usually they were paparazzi who holed up in the national forest. And sometimes people would go through our trash, looking for something they could sell on eBay – a scrap of Webb's yarn or something.

But Rafe had never done any of those things. His attention seemed to be not just harmless, but sincere. Which did me no good in my unguarded moments, when his goofy gestures made me smile. Or when my heart turned over at the sight of him. Or when, as now, he stuck close to me as we threaded our way through the crush to get to the table I'd started thinking of as ours.

I wasn't yet ready to believe that he was interested in me. But I couldn't help hoping.

"So tell me about your family," I said as soon as we were settled.

Was that panic in his eyes? "Why?" he asked.

"Well, you never talk about them. And you've met mine," I said. "Most of them, anyway."

His usual jaunty manner was back in place. "I don't think I want to meet your mother," he said.

"What? Why?"

"She seems a little intimidating."

That made me laugh. "I guess I can see that. But she's awesome. I...." I stopped myself before I said something sappy. Instead, I said, "I never knew you had a brother until today. What's he like?"

He had smirked when I paused, as if he were going to pester me until I told him what I was about to say. But when he heard the rest of it, his teasing grin fled. "He's an asshole," he said.

I blinked. Of course, I knew there were families whose members didn't get along, but I'd never before heard anyone speak as harshly about a sibling. "How, specifically? If you don't mind my asking."

He played with his paper cup, rolling it back and forth between his hands. "He just is." He glanced up at me. Then he sighed and sat back. "Okay, fine. My mother is my father's third wife. Paul is his son from his first marriage. His mother is a shrew, or so Dad has always said."

"Is she still alive?"

"Oh, yeah, she's still alive and kicking. Still making Dad's life miserable. He's still paying her alimony – she's been very careful to avoid getting married again." His lip curled in a sneer.

"Does she live in Alaska?"

"No, she's in Portland now." He hunched over his tea. "Got sick of the long, dark winters and moved back to the lower forty-eight a few years ago."

"But your brother stayed in Alaska."

"Yeah, well, that's where his job is." He glanced up at me. "He's a hydrologist. Right now, he's working on a contract with the National Park Service at Kenai Fjords."

"So he studies glaciers?" The situation was becoming a little clearer to me, but I wanted Rafe to confirm it.

"Or what's left of them, yeah. Anyway, she divorced Dad in '10. Paul was" – he cocked his head and looked at the ceiling as he ran the numbers – "four or five then. Dad married his second wife the following year, but she died of breast cancer a few months later. He started seeing Mom about a year after that, and I was born in '13."

I noted his careful phrasing. "So your parents aren't married."

"Nope." His gaze challenged me to find fault with something – or someone – in his story. Then he dropped his eyes. "I never tell anybody this stuff," he confessed.

Without thinking, I reached out and put one hand on his wrist. He slid his hand back and gripped my fingers in his. After a long moment, he sighed and released my hand. "Anyway, Paul's a lot older than me, and he's never really had time for me. When I started getting interested in science, I tried to talk to him about it, but he blew me off every time. Finally, last year, he told me to call Martin, so that's what I did. Martin said he saw promise in some of my ideas, and convinced me to transfer down here. And the rest is history." He gave me a crooked smile and took a long gulp of tea.

"What does your father do?" I asked.

"Works for a natural resources company. He spends a fair amount of time up above the Arctic Circle."

My eyes widened. "Oil drilling?"

"Oil, natural gas, whatever."

I nodded. "I gather you aren't close, then."

He barked a bitter laugh. "You could say that. I spent summers with him when I was a kid. But I grew up in Anchorage, living with Mom and her family. She works at the air force base commissary, and we lived on her salary and the annual state payments, and whatever money Dad would send us. Hardly the charmed life you've led." He drained his cup and stood up.

I couldn't let that challenge pass. I stood up, too, and blocked his exit. "My life has not been charmed," I said, trying to keep the tremor out of my voice.

He looked away from me. "Sorry," he mumbled. "I've got to go."

I didn't move. "No, you don't," I said. "Sit down. We need to talk about this."

His mouth quirked up at the corners. "You know when a woman says, 'We need to talk,' things are about to get ugly."

"They will if you won't sit down," I said, but I lightened my tone. He slid back into his chair, pushing his hair out of his eyes with one hand. I let go a sigh of relief and resumed my own seat. "Okay. Just for the record, there is nothing charming about being slated to save the world." He opened his mouth, but I held up one hand. "No, let me finish.

"Sure, I grew up with both of my parents, and my great-grandfather. I'm grateful every day for them, and for their gods, and for what they've all done on behalf of the Earth. But being part of that has a price, too." I glanced away from his rapt gaze for a moment. "I grew up in a fish bowl, Rafe. My parents argued every year over whether to homeschool Webb and me – we were a burden on the public school system, what with the enhanced security they had to put in place in case some crazy person decided to seize the building and kill us or hold us for ransom or something." I snorted. "I think they were actually relieved when the laser-eye thing started – it meant Dad could quit worrying about whether I could defend myself." I looked back at him. "But the prophecy was always there. Mom and Dad didn't ever beat me over the head with it, but it was there, just the same. Just part of the fabric of our lives." I considered this. "Or like one of Webb's yarn things. And I'm stuck to it. *Trapped* in it. I can't get out." I shook my head and took a sip of coffee that had gone cold.

"You're amazing," he said.

I shrugged, still looking at my cup. "I'm not. I'm just me." Then I looked up at him. "And at the same time, I'm supposed to be Sage the Savior. Everybody in the freaking *world* knows the gods conceived me. How do you think that makes me feel?"

Wordlessly, he took my hand.

"Sorry," I said. "I don't usually talk about this stuff." I swiped at my eyes with the heel of my free hand.

He handed me a paper napkin. "Maybe you should," he said.

"Easy to say," I said, wiping my eyes with the napkin. "But how can I tell who to trust?"

He opened his mouth and closed it. Then he gave me another crooked grin. "I'd say you can trust *me*. But that's exactly what some scumbag would say, isn't it? So how about if I just ask you to give me a chance to earn your trust."

"I can do that," I said. "If you'll let me try to earn your trust, as well."

"Oh, I already trust *you*," he said, and squeezed my hand.

I was surprised that evening when I got home to find Hilary sitting on the couch with a book. "Hey, stranger," I said as I closed the door. "We haven't seen much of you."

"Hi," she said with a little wave. "Yeah, I've been pretty busy."

Ah've.

Stop it!

I dropped my backpack on the dinette table and got a bottle of sparkling water out of the fridge. I noted while I was in there that the pile of vegetables on the bottom shelf had diminished in size. "So what's with all the cucumbers?" I asked.

"Oh!" She looked up from her book with a start. "They're for an experiment."

"What are you looking into?" I asked with a smile. "How long it takes for cucumbers to go bad in the refrigerator?"

Before Hilary could respond, Kerry breezed in the front door. "Hey, everybody. Did you guys hear?"

"Hear what?" I asked, suddenly worried. I shouldn't have had that conversation with Rafe in such a public place. Maybe some snoop had been eavesdropping. Or maybe somebody got a photo of us together, and we were tabloid fodder or something.

But no – the world did not, in fact, revolve around me. "The women's locker room in Carlson is closed for repairs," she said. "They found peepholes all over the place."

My eyes widened. "Really? Near the lockers?"

"And in the showers," Kerry said. "Thank the gods I always come home to change. I know you don't have a phys. ed. class, Sage. But Hilary, do you...?"

Hilary had flung her book aside and was halfway to the back door.

"Hilary?" I called after her, about to follow her to her room. "Is everything okay?"

She stopped and turned. Then she rushed into the kitchen, scooped up an armful of cucumbers from the bottom shelf of the fridge, and fled again down the hall. The back door slammed behind her.

Kerry and I exchanged a look. "That was weird," Kerry said.

"No shit," I said. I looked down the hall again. "You think we should follow her?"

"What for?" Kerry said with a laugh. "There's no law against carrying cucumbers around campus."

"Of course not," I said. "It was just weird, that's all." I crossed my arms and sat on the edge of the couch. "Anyway. Do the cops have any suspects?"

"Not that I heard. All I know is that they've closed the locker room 'til they can get the peepholes patched." Kerry grinned suddenly. "Maybe Hilary's going to offer them the cucumbers as patching material."

I laughed and said, "I doubt it. But there's got to be a connection." I got up and went to look out the back door.

"Do you see her?" Kerry called.

I closed the door. "Nah. She and her cucumbers are long gone."

Chapter 5

Over the next week, Security plastered the campus with handbills, asking for information about the peeping Tom in the women's locker room in Carlson. I never heard about anyone coming forward, although I did hear plenty of stupid jokes.

Two days later, a new crop of cucumbers materialized on the bottom shelf of our fridge. Hilary, however, had gone to ground again. Neither Kerry nor I ever saw her. Some nights, it looked as if she hadn't slept in her bed at all. We speculated about whether she had a guy elsewhere on campus and was using our place to make it look good for her parents.

"But then why store cucumbers in our fridge?" I asked.

"Good point," Kerry said thoughtfully. "And anyway, why would anyone go out with Hilary?"

"Oh, come on," I said. "That's unfair. There's someone out there for everyone. Except maybe me."

"Stop it," Kerry said. "You'll meet someone eventually."

"Maybe after I've saved the planet," I said gloomily, laying it on extra thick for effect. "And then he won't be able to get through the security cordon. Let's face it – I'm doomed." I let loose with a dramatic sigh.

She shook her head at me. "You're ridiculous. Look, why don't you come with me tomorrow night? There's a party at University Village. This cute guy in my social psych class invited me. We should totally go."

I regarded her steadily. "What's his name?"

"Who?"

"The guy you're trying to set me up with."

She grinned. "Mark."

That's where I thought she was going with it. "Thanks for thinking of me. Let me check my social schedule and I'll let you know."

"Oh, come *on*, Sage," she said.

I checked my phone. "Hold that protest," I told her. "I need to go meet with Dr. Raymond. We can argue some more when I get back." I grabbed my backpack and paused. "What's the other guy's name?"

"What other guy?"

"The one *you're* interested in."

She threw up her hands. "I can't slip anything past you, can I?"

I grinned at her and headed out the door.

My steps lagged as I approached Dr. Raymond's office. It occurred to me that maybe I should have coordinated arrival times with Rafe. Then it occurred to me that I'd never gotten his phone number – and in fact, I didn't know exactly where he lived.

This was all very unlike me. My mother would have been appalled. She had drilled into my head that I needed to be aware at all times of anyone I came in close contact with. It was part of the long talk we had about the conditions under which my parents would allow me to go to CU. Up to now, I had solved the problem by not getting too close to anyone – except Kerry, who, of course, they already knew.

I tried not to think about the possibility that I hadn't pressed Rafe for his number because it would imply that we were more than just classmates.

Anyway, I reasoned, if I were going to be working with him on this project of his, I would have a good excuse to get his address and phone number. That decided, I knocked on Dr. Raymond's office door.

The murmuring voices inside stopped, and Rafe himself opened the door.

"Hi. Sorry. I'm not late, am I?" I asked as I came in.

"You're right on time," said Dr. Raymond. His desk was against one wall of the narrow office; he'd spun his desk chair around so it faced a pair of mismatched guest chairs. "I guess you two already know one another."

"We do," Rafe confirmed, slouching into the chair farthest from the door. He ran his fingers through his hair, pulling back that unruly wave of his. I took the vacant chair and fought off an urge to help him with his hair.

"Good. That's a start." Dr. Raymond turned to the computer on his desk and began to make notes. "Sage, why don't you tell us what you've learned."

"I think 'learned' is probably too strong a word," I said, and launched into my story about the barbecue. "It just seems odd to me," I concluded. "I've done a little bit of research, and everything I've seen online indicates that last winter's snowpack was of a sufficient size to get us through the year in decent shape. It maybe wasn't abundant, but it was adequate. So what happened to it?"

"We don't know," Dr. Raymond said, and looked at Rafe.

"It's not just here in Colorado," Rafe said. "It's happening all over the country. All over the Northern Hemisphere. And it's happening too fast to blame it all on climate change." He nodded at Dr. Raymond. "I think there's another agent involved."

I frowned. "Agent? Like a spy, you mean?"

"Or like a god," said Rafe, watching me carefully.

Daylight dawned. "Ah," I said. "Now I get it." I stood up and hoisted my backpack onto one shoulder. "Look, I'm happy to help with any scientific aspects of your project, but I don't have a personal pipeline to the gods. And I'm not dragging my family into this."

"What about Veles?" Rafe said.

"*Now* you throw that at me?" I shot back. "It was just a dream, Rafe."

"Has He appeared to you again?" he persisted.

No, because I haven't dared to sleep without the dream helmet on since then.

"What are you two talking about?" Dr. Raymond put in. "Who is Veles?"

"The Slavic god of the underworld," Rafe said, his eyes locked on mine. "Tell him about the dream, Sage."

"I...."

"Or I will."

My mouth dropped open. I'd never seen his eyes so hard. "Fine," I said at last, punctuating the word by dropping my backpack back onto the floor. I turned to focus on Dr. Raymond, deliberately shutting Rafe out. "A few weeks ago, I dreamed I was in the mountains – not the Rockies, but somewhere else. Somewhere I didn't recognize. This huge snake slithered out from behind a rock. From what it said, it had been expecting someone named Perun. When it discovered I wasn't Him, it attacked me. So I...." I looked at the ceiling and said, really fast, "I shot a laser beam into its mouth and burned its tongue. And then I woke up," I finished.

Dr. Raymond was pretty clearly out of his depth. "Who's Perun?"

In response, Rafe pulled out his tablet and sent us each a file. I hauled out my tablet and took a look at it. "Wikipedia? Really?" I scoffed.

"It will give him the basics," he said, nodding toward our professor. "And this article is pretty well researched. Perun," he said to Dr. Raymond, "is the Slavic god of thunder. There's a myth among the Slavic peoples that Perun and Veles do battle every year as part of the change in seasons. Veles lives in Nav, at the base of the World Tree. He would climb to Prav at the top of the tree, where the gods live, and steal something belonging to Perun – His wife or His cattle, usually. Then Perun would chase Veles into our world, Yav, to get His property back, with Veles shifting into various shapes to hide from Him." He glanced at me as he said the word *shifting*. "People believed thunderstorms happened when Perun fought Veles, and lightning happened when Perun attacked Him in His hiding places. When the rain finally came, it was thought to signal Perun's victory over Veles. Then Veles would shed His skin and come back to life, and the cycle would begin again."

"So Veles is the devil?" Dr. Raymond asked. Comparative religion clearly was not his field.

"Not originally," Rafe said.

I picked it up from there. "A lot of pagan mythologies have a sort of yin-yang aspect, but the ancients didn't typically think in terms of Good versus Evil. That sort of black-and-white thinking was overlaid on a lot of cultures when Christianity conquered them. Before that, it was believed that the most important thing was for the world to be in balance – so, both darkness and light were necessary. You can still see that belief alive today in a lot of Native American cultures."

Dr. Raymond sat back and regarded us both. "Well, you two would know more about that than I would." Rafe and I exchanged a glance. "But Rafe, you've been talking about studying the possible use of glaciers as a carbon sink. What has this Veles got to do with that?"

Rafe avoided looking at me. "I think Veles may be hoarding water to force Perun into an epic battle."

Dr. Raymond raised a skeptical eyebrow. "As crazy as that sounds, let's entertain the possibility for a moment. What would this fellow stand to gain by it?"

My brain was running scenarios again, and I really didn't like what it had come up with. "Ragnarok," I blurted. "The end of the world."

Rafe nodded tightly.

"You've lost me," said Dr. Raymond.

"Okay," I said. "The gods have already told us that there are basically just three ways to fix Earth's climate. Right? We can send civilization back to the Stone Age, or we can find a way to sink the excess carbon in the atmosphere back into the ground, which I gather is what Rafe wants to study." He confirmed it with a nod, and I turned back to Dr. Raymond. "Or They can reboot the planet for us."

He frowned in concern. "But They agreed to wait for us to solve the carbon-sink issue."

"Right," Rafe said. "But that doesn't mean *every* god agreed."

"Exactly," I said. "The gods have as much trouble reaching an agreement as humans do. And They are just as likely as humans to act on their own. After all, the Second Coming never would have happened if White Buffalo Calf Pipe Woman hadn't taken matters into Her own hands." I turned to Rafe. "You think Veles has gone rogue?"

"It's the likeliest explanation I can think of," he said.

"Well, that's just great," I said in disgust. "So what do you suggest we do?"

"You could try to contact Veles again," he said.

"Oh no," I said. "Not on your life." I had a very strong recollection of how that superheated rage felt, coming off that dragon. No way was I going to invite *that* back into my head.

Rafe swallowed. "Then we need to go to Alaska."

Out of the corner of my eye, I saw Dr. Raymond nodding. "Why?" I said to Rafe, perhaps a little too harshly.

He winced, but said, "Because my brother Paul is aligned with Perun."

I threw up my hands. "Of course he is."

I could have sworn I heard White Buffalo Calf Pipe Woman laughing at me.

"I'm going to need your full name and your contact info," I told Rafe as we left Benson, where Dr. Raymond had his office.

"Why?" he asked, as he slowed to dig his phone out of the front pocket of his jeans.

I stopped to give him time to get the job done – and to admire the view, all right? "So I can book our airline tickets," I said.

He slid the phone out at last. "What do we need tickets for?"

"You said we'd have to...." My voice trailed off as I noticed his smirk. "Oh, no. No, I am not going to be doing *that* kind of flying."

"Seriously, Sage," he said. "You're going to have to try it sooner or later. It might as well be while I'm there to help you."

"My father could help me, too," I reminded him.

"But he hasn't. I bet he didn't teach you how to drive, either. I bet it was your mom."

I was surprised. He was right. "How did you...?"

"Because your mother's not a Trickster."

That wasn't precisely it. Dad knew how to drive, but he was reluctant to get behind the wheel when others were in the car. Mom said it was because he was never sure when Coyote would commandeer him. Anyway, I wasn't about to let Rafe off the hook just because he was more or less correct. "You're a Trickster, too," I reminded him.

"Yeah, but I'm not your father."

I sighed. "I'll buy the tickets."

"Aw, you're no fun," he said.

As I entered his info into my phone, I saw movement out of the corner of my eye. Something big and green was rustling the bushes next to us. "What is that?" I said.

"What's what?"

"There," I said, pointing at the corner of the building, where the green whatever-it-was rounded the corner.

Rafe ran around the end of the hedge and pelted after the vanishing figure. I followed at a slightly slower pace, and met him as he was coming back. "Lost him," he said, breathing hard.

"What was it?"

He bent forward, hands on his thighs, and shook his head. "Not sure. A little kid with a green backpack, I think. Whew, I'm out of shape."

I reviewed the memory of the glimpse I'd had. "It looked like a turtle shell to me. Was that the backpack?"

He straightened. "I think so, yeah. Weird to see a little kid on campus."

I smiled and shrugged. "Maybe he escaped from daycare. Let me go book these tickets."

"Sage." He put a hand on my shoulder to stop me. His expression was serious, although his eyes were kind. "The gods gave you the power of flight for a reason. And They sat you next to me in Water Chem for a reason. Please let me help you."

I couldn't help it – I rolled my eyes. "Now you sound like my little brother." He didn't let go, though. He just kept looking at me with those black eyes of his. "Thanks," I said finally. "If I decide to try to fly, I promise I'll come to you first."

He smiled. "I guess that will do for now." His smile faded, and for a moment I thought he might kiss me. Then he looked away, and then down – anywhere but at me. "I need to get to class. I'll see you later." And just like that, he was gone.

I stared after him for minute, my emotions whirling. Then I got a grip on myself. There were just too many variables in this situation, and I hated variables. I needed something concrete to do – something with a defined outcome.

I went back to the house to book our tickets.

I had just opened the browser when my phone rang. "Hi, Mom," I said.

"Hi, sweetheart. I finally heard back from Kurt Lange just now."

I rolled my eyes. "Classes are going great, Mom. How are you?"

"Sage, this is important. You need to listen."

I sighed and sat up. "Okay, shoot."

"Kurt knows Veles. He took his time getting back to me because he's spent the past two weeks tracking down a rumor."

"And the rumor is that Veles wants to incite a Slavic Ragnarok by challenging Perun to the thunderstorm to end all thunderstorms."

Silence. Then she said, deadpan, "I see you're way ahead of me."

"Not that far ahead," I conceded. "Rafe and I just figured it out today."

"Rafe? Oh," she said. "The guy who's allied with Raven. Your father liked him a lot."

"Good to hear," I said. My stomach got all tingly when she said it.

"Anyway," Mom went on, "what I was going to say was that you shouldn't get mixed up with Veles. It sounds like He might have gone off the deep end."

I laughed. "I didn't think gods could go crazy."

"You'd be surprised," she said. After a pause, she said, "I'm too late, aren't I?"

"Not quite yet," I assured her. "We're going to try to get in touch with Perun first. Rafe says he knows a guy."

"Be careful, sweetheart."

"I'm always careful, Mom."

Mom burst into laughter. "You sound just like your father."

If Rafe and I were going to be flying to Alaska for the weekend – and we were – I figured I'd better catch up on my studies while I had the time. So I camped out on the living room sofa and surrounded myself with actual dead-tree textbooks as well as my tablet for the rest of the afternoon.

"Wow, don't you look industrious," Kerry said as she dropped her backpack on the broken dinette chair by the door. We had been ready to throw it out, but Dad said he'd take a look at it the next time he stopped by. "Want to go out for pizza?"

"Sorry," I said, tapping the edge of my tablet. "I've got a date with a hydrologic model."

She eyed the mess I'd made. "You're not going to the party with me tomorrow night, are you?"

"Thanks for reminding me," I said, bracing my feet on the coffee table to push myself upright on the couch. "As it turns out, I have to go out of town this weekend. So, no. Sorry."

"It's okay," she said, plopping onto the other end of the couch. "Turns out Jeff isn't going to be there, anyway. Oh, did you hear?"

I smiled at her. "I've heard a lot of things. Which specific one did you mean?"

She tossed a pillow at me. "Did you hear about the commotion at the fountain?"

"No," I said. The Dalton Trumbo Fountain was in a courtyard right next to the student union. People gathered there all the time. "What happened?"

"There was a big, green turtle splashing around in it." She started fiddling with her phone.

"Turtle?" I set my tablet aside.

"Yeah. Somebody posted it to Instapic." She handed over her phone. Sure enough, there was the kid with the backpack – except it didn't look like a backpack in the picture. Someone had captioned it, *CU's own Teenage Mutant Ninja Turtle!*

I squinted at the photo. "Is that Hilary in the background?"

Kerry took back her phone. "It is!" She grinned at me. "Good eye. I didn't notice her before." She took another look at the photo. "Boy, she doesn't look happy, does she?"

"No," I said thoughtfully. "No, she really doesn't."

Chapter 6

I am here to tell you that I will never do a weekend trip to Seward, Alaska, ever again. Between travel time there and back, we had only about twenty-four hours on the ground – and we spent five of them doing the round-trip drive from Anchorage to Seward.

It would have been quicker if I'd been able to afford tickets on the hypersonic plane from Denver to Seattle. But I couldn't. Even two regular tickets ate up most of my allowance for the semester.

Rafe's mother, Sadie Hanlon, picked us up from the airport in Anchorage Friday night. She told me to call her Auntie, which I was okay with because she reminded me of my great-aunt Hannah: big-hearted, but with an inner core of pure iron. She fussed over Rafe, which was hilarious because he clearly hated it, and fed us a late supper of salmon and rice.

She shook her head when she learned what we planned to do the next day. "Paul has never given you the time of day," she said to Rafe. "What makes you think he'll help you now?"

"He has to," said Rafe. "And anyhow, all he needs to do is point me in the right direction. Which he's done before."

"When was that?" she said, hands on her hips.

"When he sent me to Martin in Colorado."

"He sent you to Colorado to get rid of you," Auntie said.

Rafe scowled and bent his head over his dinner. He'd been so insistent on us coming that I never questioned it. But now, I began to wonder whether we were on a fool's errand.

We dropped his mother off at work before sunrise the next morning and drove her car the two-and-a-half hours to Seward. Travel books, I have since learned, call this the most beautiful drive in all of Alaska, and they are not far off the mark. Stunning scenery surrounded us – lakes, marshland, and snowcapped mountains. I nearly got whiplash from the view. Rafe found my reaction highly entertaining.

Seward was a picturesque town on Resurrection Bay – part quaint fishing village, part tourist trap. The shops were crawling with people from the lower forty-eight. Many of them had cruised up the Inside Passage and were now headed inland on buses to see Mt. McKinley. Others had taken the Alaska Railroad down from

Anchorage for the day in the hopes of seeing a whale from the deck of a catamaran.

Rafe knew how to avoid most of crowds. We drove up into the mountains overlooking the bay and headed for the Kenai Fjords visitor center to ask after his brother.

"He's out on the ice," the ranger on duty told us. He had recognized Rafe from his job there the previous summer. "We don't expect him back for a couple of days."

"We don't have that long. We're flying back to Denver tomorrow. Could you radio him for us?"

"It needs to be an emergency," said the ranger, shaking his head. "You know the rules, Rafe. I'm sorry."

Rafe nodded. "That's okay. Thanks anyway." He motioned to me and we stepped outside. There, he grabbed my hand and led me to the side of the lodge – away from the tourist hordes that had come to see a real, live glacier.

"So we came all this way for nothing?" I hissed at him. "I spent a ton of money on those last-minute tickets, you know." Then I noticed the look in his eye – and then I remembered when I'd seen it before. "Oh, no," I said, backing off a step.

He nodded. "Oh, yes. We'll have to fly."

"No."

"It's the only way to get up where Paul is."

"No!"

"It'll be a very short flight. Just a couple of minutes." I recognized that wheedling tone, too. It was the same one Webb used on me when he wanted me to do one of his chores for him.

I planted my feet and crossed my arms. "What part of 'no' do you not get?"

"Look. I'll level with you." He put one hand against the side of the building and leaned over me – a good trick, as we were nearly the same height. Quietly, he said, "My mother was right. My asshole of a brother isn't going to give me the time of day. He hates my mother because she's an Alaskan Native, and he hates my father for sleeping with her. As far as he's concerned, the world would be better off if I didn't exist."

I blinked. "I thought all the Neanderthals had died out."

He snorted. "All but him."

"I'm sorry, Rafe," I said. Some of the fight drained out of me. "I can't imagine what that must be like."

"You misunderstand me," he said. "That's not the point. He won't talk to me, but he'll talk to *you*."

I blinked again. "I'm Native American, too, you know," I reminded him.

"But you're not related to him," he said. "And you're a girl."

I let out a *whoof* as I leaned back against the building. "And here I thought my family was complicated." I looked at him sidelong. "We can't hike out to him, huh?"

"Not and catch our flight tomorrow."

"You knew it was going to turn out like this, didn't you?" I said, and sighed. "Never mind. What do I do with my clothes?"

It was his turn to look surprised. "Clothes? What do you mean?"

"Dad always has to take his off when he shifts."

"Wow. *That's* inconvenient."

I snorted. "You have no idea."

He regarded me with a mischievous look. Then he sobered. "No, I can't do that to you. This is too important. Look. The last time you flew, did you need to undress?"

"I didn't even know I'd done it," I began. "I was asleep when it happened, and…. No. I was still wearing my pajamas when I woke up."

"Okay." He looked relieved. "Then you should be fine."

"But how do I…?" I raised my hands helplessly.

"How did you do it last time?" he asked patiently.

"I don't know!" I shouted. "I was asleep!"

"Easy," he said, pushing one hand at me. "Keep it down or we'll have an audience."

With a guilty glance behind me, I shut up.

"Let's try it this way," he went on. "What were you thinking about when you shifted? Or dreaming about?"

"I dreamed I was flying," I said.

He nodded. "Okay. I can work with that. Come here." He took my hand again and led me up an unmarked trail that wound away from the lodge and dead-ended at what looked like a maintenance shed. From there, we moved deeper into the pine forest.

"Aren't we supposed to stay on the trail?" I asked.

"Shhh."

We didn't walk very far, but suddenly I felt as if we had entered a primeval forest. He came to a halt and turned to me. "Feel that?"

I nodded. "It's like we're in a time of no time." And just like that, my rational brain kicked in. "This isn't going to work. We should go back."

"You're just scared," he said. "Close your eyes."

"Why?"

"Sage." His patience was wearing thin. "Just do it."

"What are you going to do to me?"

"Nothing!" He let out a frustrated groan and walked away from me. "Why do you have to be so fucking difficult?"

"*I'm* difficult?" I yelled. A white-hot sensation was building behind my eyes, but at that moment I hardly cared whether he went up in smoke. "This whole trip was *your* idea! You *knew* it wasn't going to work, but you talked me into coming anyway!" The heat inside me was building, overspilling the reservoir behind my eyes and flooding into my core. "And contrary to popular belief, I'm not made of money. I spent my expense money for the *whole semester* on those tickets!" The blaze was shooting down my arms and legs now, and my hands felt as if they were on fire. "And now I find out that you tricked me! You planned this whole thing to get me to fly, didn't you? Well, it's too bad for you, because *I'm not going to do it!*"

"Methinks she doth protest too much," he said from below me.

Below me?

Sure enough, I was airborne. My arms had sprouted flaming feathers and were undulating just enough to keep me aloft.

"Goddamn you, Rafe Orloff!" I screeched. At my cry, the other birds in the forest erupted in alarm. "You tricked me!"

It's what I do best, he said in my head. His smirk came through loud and clear. *Come on, Paul is this way.* And Rafe the Raven flew up and out of the clearing, until he was just a speck against the blue of the sky.

Wait! I cried, and moved my arms faster. I shot up so fast that I nearly collided with him where he'd paused to let me catch up.

Hey now, he said, cartwheeling away from me. *Slow down. Take your time to get used to it.*

Treading air again, I looked down – and forgot my anger. *Holy shit.* The blue-white glaciers of the Kenai Peninsula, and their ever-widening rim of jagged cliffs, stretched out before me. I could even see the Aleutian Islands curving away from us in the far distance.

Beautiful, huh? said the proud native son, as he flew slow circles around me. *Is it worth the subterfuge?*

I'm reserving judgment. I tried to glare at him, but I couldn't tell if he got it. I wasn't sure whether I could glare effectively in this form without shooting sparks from my eyes. *Where's your brother?*

This way. With an audible cry, he headed off to the right at a sedate pace.

I found that flying was a lot like walking, in that the mechanics were hardwired into my physical form. If I thought about it too much, I'd miss a beat and tangle myself up. But if I forgot about trying to fly, and concentrated on staying even with Rafe, it went fine.

It was only a few minutes later when Rafe said, *That's his camp,* and began circling for the descent. I followed, noticing for the first time the trail of smoke I was leaving in my wake. This form could cover some ground in a hurry, but it was going to be useless for sneaking up on anyone.

Although why that thought had occurred to me, I had no idea. As lovely as the view was, I intended to maintain my personal no-fly rule. Rafe had tricked me into shifting this time, but it wasn't going to happen again.

A four-season tent was pitched on the ice below us. Several meters further on, a man in serious cold-weather gear – parka, face mask, and boots with crampons – knelt on the glacier. He was fiddling with a long, slender probe, patiently working it back and forth, trying to push it down into the ice.

That's Paul? I asked Rafe. *He's a moron. Why isn't he using a power tool?*

Too cold for battery power, Rafe said. *And too much friction will melt the ice and screw up his reading.* He dipped a wing slightly toward the tent. *I'll wait over there. I don't want him to see me.*

Hey! But apparently Rafe's mind was made up. I was on my own with the surlier Orloff brother. Muttering under my breath, I spiraled down to land.

As soon as my feet touched the ice, I realized I'd never asked my annoying companion how to get out of this get-up. But I needn't have worried. Heat had transformed me, and now ice was doing the job in reverse. In a moment, I was back to myself – and hardly dressed for the subzero cold that hit me in my human face like a slap. With an effort, I dialed the heat back up again. Then I trudged in my hiking boots to meet my doom, leaving a trail of smoking footprints behind me.

"Mr. Orloff?" I called when I was within a couple of yards of him.

He did a classic double-take, and scrambled to his feet. "Who are...how did you...you're going to die out here dressed like that!" His voice was muffled from the insulated cocoon he'd wrapped himself in, but his shock was unmistakable through the goggles that shielded his eyes.

"Hi, Mr. Orloff," I said. "Sorry to have startled you. My name is Sage Curtis, and I need to talk to Perun."

"Who?" He was looking me up and down, evidently trying to figure out how I'd materialized before him and why I hadn't turned into a popsicle yet. Then he pointed to my feet in horror. "You're melting the ice!"

I looked down. Sure enough, my feet were sinking into the glacier. "Sorry," I said again, and dialed down the heat a bit.

"Get away from here!" he yelled. "You'll ruin my readings!"

I put my hands out before me. "No worries, sir, I'll be out of your hair in just a moment. I just need to know how to contact Perun, that's all."

"Go away!" he yelled, and started toward me with one gloved fist raised.

Just as I took a step back, a puffin came out of nowhere and flew straight at my attacker's face. With another yell, the man raised his arms to ward off the crazed bird, stumbled backward, and landed on his ass on the ice.

The puffin made another circuit to make sure the guy stayed down. I rolled my eyes. "Dad," I said. "You didn't have to come. Rafe and I have got this."

"Rafe?" the man said in disbelief, turning his head from side to side. "My *brother* Rafe? Where is he? When I get my hands on that kid...."

In another second or two, the puffin's colorful head morphed into my father's gray-haired human one. "He's not a kid, Mr. Orloff, and neither is my daughter. They're here on a mission to benefit humanity, and we would all appreciate your cooperation."

"And who the hell are you?"

"Joseph Curtis. I'd shake your hand, but...." Dad gave a little wave with his right wing. "It wouldn't work very well. Sorry. And I apologize for knocking you down."

"Dad," I tried again, "we've got this. How did you find me, anyway?"

He pivoted his neck to give me a stern look. "The credit card company called your mother about the charge for your airline tickets."

Whoops.

"Just call Perun for us. Please, Paul." That was Rafe, human again, and trudging up to us. His arms were locked across his chest. I swore I could hear his teeth chattering.

"Rafe, so help me," Paul said. He scrambled to his feet and took a step toward his brother. "If you and your friends have ruined my experiment, I'll...." He left the threat hanging, apparently unable to come up with a sufficiently dire penalty. Instead, he said, "I'm dealing with delicate instruments here!"

While he was yelling at Rafe, I took a better look at his equipment. "By any chance," I asked, "is this glacier melting with no appreciable runoff?"

Paul spun on his heel to face me. "How did you know that?"

"Because the same thing has been happening in the Rockies," I said.

"And in G-greenland," said Rafe. His teeth really were chattering now. "A-and in the I-italian A-a-alps. And in S-s-s-siberia."

I couldn't let him become a popsicle, could I? "Put your hands in your armpits," I told him, and put my arms around him.

"T-thanks," he said.

His face was inches from mine. "Better?"

"Yeah. Much." He rested his freezing forehead against mine and breathed out in relief.

My father chose that moment to clear his throat. "As your brother was saying, Mr. Orloff, the world seems to be losing track of its water."

"Which is impossible," Paul said, apparently preferring to talk with a human-headed puffin than acknowledge that his brother and I were here. "Earth is a closed system. The gods said so. The water must be going somewhere."

"We think we know where it's going," I said. "Veles has it."

Paul barked a laugh. "Veles?"

"Yes, Veles. That's why we need to talk to Perun." Rafe wasn't warm yet, by any stretch of the imagination, but at least his lips weren't blue any more. "Please just call him for us, okay?"

A sharp clap of thunder rent the air. "There's no need," said a new, masculine voice. And Perun the Slavic thunder god strode up to us.

I mean, it had to be Him. He rocked the look: copper-colored beard, fur robe, leather boots. An axe covered in Viking knotwork that reminded me of Thor's hammer was stuck in His belt. At least He'd avoided the dopey horned helmets the Norse gods wore.

"Perun," Dad and I said at the same time. We stopped and looked at one another. I'm pretty sure my eyes were close to molten. His were wide with surprise.

"Dad," I said, trying not to sound too threatening, "we've got this." *Shut up and let me handle it!*

He threw up a wing and retreated.

"Perun," I began again, "thank You for coming. We have reason to believe that Veles is hoarding the world's water in order to force a showdown with You."

The god's face had grown steadily darker. "He dares to steal the lifeblood of Our planet?" He banged the haft of His axe against the palm of His other hand. "I will give Him a battle He will never forget!"

"No!" Rafe said. "That's exactly what He wants You to do!"

"If You play into His hands on this," I said, "You could destroy the world."

Perun was nodding. "Yes. That's how it works. We fight, and then it rains. And then the Earth is renewed and the cycle begins again."

"There will be no new cycle," I said, stepping toward Him. "Not this time. Not if You fight Veles on His terms."

"Does the word Ragnarok mean anything to You?" Dad said.

I shot him a murderous look. *Butt out, damn it!*

But Perun's eyes had widened in surprise. Clearly, He did know what it meant. Now He was stroking His beard thoughtfully. "I see," He said. "Yes, I see." He looked at me. "But the Earth needs water. What can we do?"

"Maybe there's another way," Rafe said.

"What way?" Perun asked.

"I don't know yet," Rafe said. "I need to think about it. We" – he put an arm around my shoulders – "need to talk it over."

I moved my arms to his waist and gave him an extra shot of warmth. It might not have been entirely deliberate.

"We *all* need to talk it over," Dad said. "The world will be okay for another few days, unless Veles seriously steps up His game, and we have no reason to believe He will do so." At last, he deferred to Rafe and me. "Right?"

"Not that I know of," Rafe said.

"Okay. Then let's let these...." He was about to call us *kids*, but lucky for him, he caught himself in time. "Let's let these young people go back home and get back to class. We can reconvene in a few days with all of the pantheons, and figure out what we need to do to stop this from turning into the end of the world. All right?" Dad looked around the circle.

"I will let My people know," Perun said.

"Naomi will have White Buffalo Calf Pipe Woman pass the word," Dad said.

"We'll be there," I said firmly, and Rafe nodded.

Dad gave me a sidelong look, but he said okay.

Paul, who was clearly out of his depth, spoke up. "Are we done here? Can I get back to work?"

Perun stepped between Paul and Rafe, watching them both. "Paul," He said gently, "have you so many people who love you that you can afford to reject your brother?"

For the first time, Paul looked chagrined.

"Be kind to him," Perun advised him as He stowed His axe in His belt. "Someday you will have need of one another." The god rested one hand on Paul's well-insulated shoulder, and put His other hand on Rafe's shoulder. Then He nodded at Dad and me. "Until then." And He faded away.

Paul shot Rafe a dirty look.

"We're going, we're going," said Rafe, as he stepped away from both of us, giving himself room to shift. Then he looked at me, concerned. "Will you be okay?"

I reached for the fire that I'd banked within me, and it flared to life. "Coming," I said with a grin. I glanced at my father, my smile fading. "Dad?"

"I'll see you at home," was all he said. But I recognized the tone of voice and cringed inwardly. His head shrank back to puffin dimensions, and he took wing.

With a look full of regret for Paul, Rafe shifted and followed my father.

"Um. Nice to meet you," I said to Paul, who was regarding me silently, his expression unreadable. "Sorry again." Still nothing.

I gave up, and let the fire fill me and lift me into the sky.

Chapter 7

By the time we got back to Anchorage, Rafe and I were both exhausted. We had just enough energy to nuke something quick from Fred Meyer for dinner, shovel it in, and head for bed. I swear I was asleep before my head hit the pillow.

Auntie made us breakfast the next morning. "So," she said as she dished up salmon and eggs, "did you get what you came for?"

"I think so," Rafe told her. "We'll know after the gods meet in a few days."

"And we are going to be there," I said firmly.

He looked up at me, surprised. "Was there any doubt?"

"You don't know my parents," I said. "If they can keep me out of the process, they'll do it, in the name of protecting me." I put air quotes around *protecting*.

"Looks to me like you can take care of yourself," Auntie said.

"Thank you," I said, with a grateful smile. "Feel free to tell them that."

Her mischievous grin rivaled her son's. "Maybe I will."

I was still pretty tired by the time we got on the plane, so I expected to sleep the whole way home. But I was too keyed up.

Rafe was antsy, too. He tried to watch a movie, but he kept fiddling with the headphones the airline had given him. Finally he gave up and stowed them in the seat back pocket. "Busted," he informed me.

"Want mine?"

"Nah."

"You could ask for another pair."

"No, it's fine. I've seen that movie already, anyway." He stared out the window for a few minutes.

Meanwhile, I was screwing up the courage to talk about something that had been bugging me since Saturday morning. Finally, I said, "Can I ask you something?"

Almost too quickly, he turned back to me. "What?"

"Outside the visitor center at Kenai Fjords," I said. "Did you deliberately get me angry?"

"You mean, so you would…" He raised his hand toward the ceiling, fluttering his fingers.

"Yeah."

He dropped his hand back to his lap and let out a breath. "It wasn't deliberate. I mean, I didn't hatch some brilliant plan ahead of time to get you fired up. But when you started to get mad, I saw these little dots of red in your eyes."

"And you figured it was working," I said. "So you went with it."

"Pretty much, yeah." He was silent for a few seconds. "So did you know they do that?"

"Did I know my eyes turn red when I'm mad? Oh, yeah," I said with a self-conscious laugh. "Webb likes to see how far he can push me before they ignite."

He laughed softly. "Brothers, huh?" His smile faded, and he looked out the window again.

After a moment, I said, "You were right, for what it's worth. He's an asshole."

He snorted without turning back to me. "Yeah."

I studied him: the high cheekbones, the hawk nose. The lips I didn't want to think about, so of course I couldn't stop thinking about them. The arm that I wanted him to put around my shoulders again, the way he had on the glacier the day before.

My mother didn't raise any reticent children. I don't know whether it was due to her training as a mediator or her experiences in dealing with the gods, or whether it was just who she was, but she had drilled it into us that if we wanted something, we needed to be direct. No waffling. No mincing words. "You'll never get it if you don't ask," she'd say.

And I had very little experience with men, at least in terms of dating. So I didn't know I was supposed to flutter my eyelashes and act all winsome, and wait for the guy to make a move. Well, okay, I'd heard about that junk, but it seemed pretty pointless to me. I wanted Rafe to put his arm around me. There was only one thing in the way – and to my mind, it was an easy fix.

"Can we just…." I squirmed around in my seat until I got my right hand under the armrest between us and began pushing it up, out of the way. When he figured out what I was doing, he moved his elbow and helped me stow the divider.

"Better?" he asked, as we resituated ourselves. "More room now."

"More comfy," I said. "It was digging into my side." Which was only mostly untrue.

"Sorry," he said.

"Not your fault."

"No, I mean, it was bugging me, too. I should have moved it before. I would have…except…." He never finished the sentence. Instead, with a tentative motion, he slipped his arm around my shoulders.

I laid my head on his shoulder and closed my eyes. "You should have done that before, too."

"Yeah?" His breath was warm in my ear.

"Yeah."

I looked up at him, and he kissed me.

As soon as we changed planes in Seattle, the armrest was stowed immediately, by mutual agreement.

I walked in our front door to the sound of the TV blaring. Kerry sat on the couch with her homework spread out on the coffee table, but she was devoting more attention to the guy whose arms were draped around her.

"Hi, everybody," I yelled over the TV.

Kerry grabbed the remote and dialed down the sound. "Hey, roomie," she said.

I looked at the guy. "And you are…?"

"This is Jeff," Kerry said.

Jeff looked to be of medium height, although was hard to tell for sure, the way he was slouching on the sofa. He had sharp, almost pixie-ish features, and his hairdo was very trendy: he'd sculpted it with some kind of gunk that made it meet in the center of his skull. Some guys could rock the look, but it made Jeff look like he had a pointy head. He also looked half-stoned. "Hey, roomie," he said, with a little wave.

I shot Kerry an *oh no he isn't* look.

She got the picture. "Hey, I'm starving," she told him. "Let's go get something to eat. And then maybe we can study some more at your place." The way she stroked his tattooed arm, I got the feeling that *study* was a euphemism for something else.

"Well, now, don't be rude," he said. "You didn't ask Roomie if she wanted to come. Maybe she's hungry, too." He gave me a smile that I guessed was meant to be sexy, but it just made him look even more like a stoner.

"No, that's okay," I said. "Roomie has had a very long and tiring weekend, and is planning to eat some cereal and head to bed." And I rolled my suitcase down the hall to my room and shut the door.

About five minutes later, Kerry knocked and let herself in. "He's gone," she said. "Isn't he adorable?" She giggled like a high schooler.

"Honestly?" I said. "He looks like he's on drugs."

"We had a smoke." She plopped on my bed.

I shot her a dubious look. "You can't perfect that look on just one smoke."

"Well," she said with a self-conscious laugh, "maybe it was more than one."

I shook my head. "I thought he wasn't going to go to that party on Friday."

"He didn't," she said, as she hugged one of my pillows. "But we hung out all day yesterday and today. Don't be judgy. He's really a cool guy." She put the pillow down and smoothed the top with one hand. "So how was your weekend? Was it as fabulous as mine?"

"I don't think I'd call it fabulous," I said. "Interesting, maybe. And exhausting. If I'd known how long it takes to fly to Anchorage, I wouldn't have…."

"So what's his name?" she broke in.

I tried not to look too dreamy. "It's Rafe. You met him at the pizza place."

"Oh my gods!" she crowed. "You're in love!"

"What? No. Stop. It's not like that."

But she was already headed out the door. "Maybe it's not like that yet, but I bet it will be," she said in a sing-song voice. "I need to talk to Webb."

"Leave him out of this!" I yelled after her. It was bad enough that I kept remembering the way my all-knowing brother had looked at Rafe and me. I didn't need Kerry to pump him for details.

She did get hold of Webb. I knew that for a fact. But she refused to tell me what he said to her. And of course, Webb himself wasn't about to share any of the juicy details about my future with me. But every now and then, Kerry would look at me with an odd, speculative expression – almost as if she was afraid.

Kerry was my best friend. Now she was scared of me.

Have I mentioned how much I hate being Sage the Savior?

I barely saw Rafe at all that week. On Monday, he begged off on our regular coffee date after Water Chem so he could get caught up on his homework. Going out of town had put him behind the eight ball, he said.

On Wednesday, he bailed again. Well, okay, I thought. He *could* conceivably be that far behind.

But on Friday, he tried it again. More homework, he said. Still not caught up, he said.

"Bullshit," I said. "Come on, Rafe. What's going on?"

He ducked his head. "I just...I dunno. Maybe this is all happening too fast."

"*What's* happening too fast?" I said, dismayed. Rafe was the first guy I'd ever been interested in who wasn't fazed by what my mother calls the woo-woo stuff – because he lived with it daily, too. If *he* ran away from me, I irrationally believed, then I might never find anyone. Which is not a message that a nineteen-year-old woman is ready to hear. "Nothing happened last weekend," I went on in a rush. "I mean, nothing happened between *us*. Physically." I wasn't exactly setting records for clarity myself, which irritated me.

"No. I know. It's just...." He still wouldn't look at me.

Now I was getting seriously annoyed. "I can't fix it unless I know what it is," I said, trying to keep the edge out of my voice.

At last, he looked at me. "There's nothing to fix," he said, sounding a little surprised. "I just need.... Hey, did you see that?" Something had apparently caught his eye over my shoulder.

"Don't even try it." I planted my feet and glared at him.

Apparently, he hadn't heard me. "I bet it's that kid again!" He hurdled the hedge and took off.

"Rafe!" I threw up my hands and ran after him.

Sure enough, it was the critter with the backpack, or shell, or whatever. And this time, Rafe was not going to let it get away. He shifted and flew like an arrow at the little fellow, using his talons to grab the top of the medallion shape at the nape of its neck. The collision knocked the critter off-balance and it fell on its belly in the scrubby grass between the Aerospace and Electrical Engineering buildings. Rafe landed squarely on its back and squawked madly as I finally caught up.

"I've got it," I said, breathing hard. "Move over." I knelt in the wet grass and lay crosswise atop it so Rafe could shift back. Its face was turned toward me, giving me a clear view of its duck-like bill. The thing we had mistaken for a backpack was rock-hard – like a turtle shell – and its face and neck were a mottled green.

Wait a minute. Wet grass? But we haven't had rain for weeks! What the hell?

The critter gabbled something in a language I didn't recognize. Rafe, however, did. *"Eigo o hanasemasu ka?"* he said.

"Iie!" the critter said, with what sounded for all the world like an evil laugh.

I regarded Rafe with surprise. "What did you say to him?"

"I asked him if he spoke English, and he said no."

And laughed like a maniac. "Terrific. Which language *does* he speak?"

"Oh! Japanese."

I blinked. "I didn't know you spoke Japanese."

He grinned. "I don't, really. But Mom has a pretty big anime collection, and I watched them all the time, growing up. I got so I could pick out a few words here and there."

"Enkou-san!" a female voice called. And here came Hilary Takahashi after us, a cucumber in each petite fist.

The critter growled something at her. Her mouth dropped into a perfect *O*, and she simultaneously bowed while shrugging out of her backpack and digging out a water bottle. "You can get off of him," she said to me. "He can't go anywhere right now."

"Hilary," I said as I stood and brushed off my wet knees, "you have got some 'splaining to do."

She paused in the act of unscrewing the cap on the bottle. "This is Enkou," she said, indicating the prostrate ninja turtle. "He's a kappa."

"Okay," I said slowly. "What's a kappa?"

"Japanese water demon," said Rafe, a look of wonder on his face. "I never thought I'd see a real one."

"Enkou's not a demon!" said Hilary. "He's just…."

"Trouble," I said, looking down at the critter, who was muttering to itself.

Understanding dawned on Rafe's face. "The kind of trouble that causes a stir by taking a bath in the Dalton Trumbo Fountain," he said. His expression turned suspicious. "And the kind that drills peepholes in the walls of the women's locker room."

"Please don't tell," Hilary begged us. "He's promised not to do it any more."

"Yeah, but has he promised to do it any less?" Rafe asked with a manic grin.

"It's not funny!" she cried. "I can't help it that he followed me to college! He's mischievous by nature!"

"Oh, great," I groaned. "Another freaking Trickster. That's exactly what I needed in my life."

Rafe wiggled his eyebrows at me.

"I'm sorry," Hilary said. "I've been trying to keep him out of the way, but I can't keep an eye on him 24/7. I have to go to class sometimes." She sounded defensive.

"Hotaru-chan!" the kappa yelled, and followed it with a string of cranky Japanese that caused her to start bowing again.

"Help me with him," she said to us. "I have to get him upright so I can pour the water on his head." For the first time, I noticed the kappa's haircut resembled a tonsure, with a concave bald spot in the middle.

"Are you sure you want to do that?" asked Rafe as he lent a hand. The beast muttered something. "Hey!" Rafe said to it, offended, and Hilary scolded it in its native tongue.

"What's the deal with the water?" I asked.

"It allows him to walk on land," Hilary said as the lifted the kappa to its hind feet. "If the water pours out, he's stuck. Paralyzed."

I glanced down at my knees. *So that's how the grass got wet. The water spilled out when Rafe knocked him down.*

"He could even die," she was saying.

I cocked an eyebrow at her. "And the downside would be…?"

I was trying to make a joke, but she looked as if I'd struck her. "Enkou's my friend!" she protested. "And he's very loyal." To Rafe, she said, "Keep hold of him." Then she opened the water bottle and poured the contents into the depression on top of the critter's head. It closed its eyes in relief, and she chattered to it in Japanese.

"*Hai, hai, hai,*" it said, its shoulders sagging.

She gave it a cucumber and said, "It's okay. You can let go now. He's promised to behave."

Rafe dropped Enkou's arm as the critter began to devour his snack. "So where's he living?" he asked Hilary.

"Boulder Creek," she said. "But it's very low. There's been so little rain."

"Yeah, we know," I said.

Rafe looked thoughtful. "I wonder," he said, his voice trailing off. Then he looked at me. "When's that big meeting, anyway?"

"An excellent question," I said. I hadn't heard a word from my parents since our return from Alaska. It wasn't like them to be this quiet. Which meant I'd been right – they were freezing Rafe and me out of the planning for Veles's takedown. "I think I need to call home. Right now."

"I'll come with you," he said. "You should come, too, Hilary. And bring Enkou. I have a feeling we'll need him before this is all over."

I looked at each of them in turn while I thought about what Rafe had just said. "You know," I said, "you might very well be right."

Chapter 8

We must have been quite a sight as we walked to the house. More than one person asked us where the Halloween party was. But Enkou kept his word. He trudged along next to Hilary almost meekly, and seemed oblivious to the comments.

Which gave me time to mull over what had just happened. Rafe had been about to pull away from me – I was sure of it. Part of me wanted to finish that conversation, another part of me wanted to just let it go and hope it would blow over, and still another part of me wanted to run away from all these squishy feelings and hide under the nearest rock.

Then the whole thing with Enkou happened, and now he was on fire to come to my house and talk to my parents. So maybe he considered our...whatever it was...to be task-based only? Or maybe he wanted to wrap up this thing with Veles so he could break up with me as soon as it was over? Well, okay, not break up. We would have to have a relationship before we could break up.

I risked a look at him. His mouth was set in a determined line, but his eyes sparkled with excitement. He must have felt my eyes on him, because he glanced down at me and gave me a one-armed hug.

What the hell? One minute he's pulling away, and now he's all cuddly!

Ambiguity was never my strong suit. I hugged him back, briefly, and dropped my arm. A couple of seconds later, his arm fell away.

To keep from making myself crazy over my relationship-or-not with Rafe, I forced my thoughts into a channel I knew more about: my parents.

It would be easy enough for them to hide preparations for the meeting with the gods from me – I was thirty minutes away at college. But they couldn't hide anything from Webb. For one thing, he was really good at hearing conversations he wasn't meant to hear. He'd certainly heard enough things that *I'd* tried to keep from him. For another, well, he was Webb. Nothing got past him unless it had to do with him personally. So all I had to do was get him on Skype and either entice him with something he wanted or blackmail him with something he didn't want. It had always worked in the past, and I had no reason to believe it wouldn't work again.

Our entourage startled Kerry and Jeff, who were on the couch when we entered through the front door. They must have been pretty far into their make-out session – Kerry wore a guilty look as she adjusted her clothing and kicked her bra under the edge of the couch. Jeff still looked stoned. "Hey, everybody," he said with a wave. Then he saw Enkou, and his eyes opened wider than I'd ever seen them. "Whoa. Cool costume. Where's the Halloween party?"

"It's been done," I said tiredly.

"It's not a costume," Hilary told him. "This is Enkou. He's a kappa."

"What's a kappa?"

"Japanese water…god." Rafe caught Hilary's glare, and self-edited his comment just in time.

"Whoa," said Jeff again, with a pleased grin. "That's pretty cool. I've never met a god before."

"Clearly," I said. Then a thought occurred to me. Maybe we wouldn't need to talk to Webb, after all. "Hey, Kerry, has Epona said anything to you about a big meeting of the gods?"

"Epona?" Jeff asked. "Is that your mom?"

Kerry ignored him. "Haven't heard from Her in days."

I sighed. "It was worth a try. Come on, guys." I led the way to my room.

Kerry followed us, with Jeff trailing her. "What's going on?" she asked. So I gave her the short version of events, noting that Jeff looked more and more confused. Finally I asked, "Does he need to be here?"

"Oh, I'm not leaving now," he said. "This is just getting good."

I rolled my gaze toward the ceiling and went to fire up Skype.

Rafe stood to my right. Hilary and Enkou were to my left, and Kerry and Jeff stood behind them. In a moment, Webb appeared across from us in living virtual 3D. "Wow," he said. "You brought your posse. Hi, Kerry. Hi, Rafe. Hi, all the people I don't know."

I did a quick round of introductions. Then I asked, "Are Mom and Dad around?"

He looked shifty-eyed. "Not right at the moment, no."

"Shit," I said under my breath. Aloud, I said with a sweet smile, "Webb, my dearest darling brother…."

He made a comical face to the others. "Here it comes."

I kept going. "Would you please tell me something?"

He rubbed his hands together. "It depends on what it's worth to you."

He was enjoying this way too much. But I was too far into it now to quit. "All I want to know is this: When is the big meeting with the gods?"

He winced. "Alas, dearest darling sister. I can tell you anything but that."

"Anything?" said Rafe with a mischievous grin.

I pushed at Rafe with one hand to shush him. "Why?" I asked Webb.

"Seriously?" Webb said with a cackle. "Because they told me not to tell you."

"And that's relevant how?"

He sighed. "I suppose it doesn't matter. They're not having it here anyway."

"Where's it going to be, then?" Then it clicked. They were going to meet in the Otherworld – the gods' world, where Mom had mediated the agreement that led to the Second Coming. "Oh, shit. That's not fair. I don't know how to get there."

"I expect that's why they picked it," Webb said.

"When?" I asked. "Come on, Webb, tell me. I'll pay you."

"Actually," he said, glancing at the time in the corner of his screen, "it ought to be starting right about now."

I groaned in frustration. "Damn it! They can't shut us out! This is *our* project!"

Even as I railed against my overprotective parents, my brain was clicking through the options. Which god could I ask to take us there? Maybe Epona. "Kerry?" I asked.

She shook her head. "She's going to side with your mom and dad. You know that."

I turned back to Webb's image, thinking aloud. "Thor probably won't return my call. What about Grandfather?"

"He's with Mom and Dad."

"Of course he is." I sighed. "Rafe, do you think Perun would help us?"

"Maybe," he said. "If you can figure out how to contact Him without flying back up to Alaska. And Raven doesn't seem inclined to give us a hand with anything right now." He grimaced. Then he gestured toward the kappa. "Enkou's a god. Maybe he could get us there." He looked inquiringly at Hilary.

She shrugged, and spoke to Enkou with a bow. After a quick conversation, she shook her head. "He says he could get himself there, but he's not strong enough to take anyone else."

"Well, that's it. We're stuffed." I plopped down on the edge of my bed. All the years I'd spent distancing myself from my family heritage were coming back to bite me in the ass.

"Hey, Webb," said Kerry with a giggle, "maybe you could make us a magic slingshot." Jeff chuckled and licked her ear. She giggled again and flinched away. "Hey, cut it out," she said, batting her eyelashes at him. "This is serious."

"Magic slingshot," he said, still chuckling. "That's hilarious. *You're* hilarious." He put his arms around her and started nuzzling her neck.

"Jeff, I mean it," Kerry said. She cringed a little, but she didn't push him away.

"Kerry," I said in warning, but of course it was too late. Webb had seen the whole thing.

Stone-faced, he said, "I have to go." His hand reached out to end the call.

"Wait!" I said. I don't know what I thought I was doing. It's not as if I could have made it any better – I was too far away to give him a hug, which is about all I could offer him, and it wouldn't have don't any good anyway. But he heard me, and paused. And at that moment, someone began to materialize next to Rafe.

"Mom!" he said.

"Auntie?" I asked in disbelief. I wouldn't have recognized her if Rafe hadn't said anything to her. She wore the pelt of a grizzly and a wooden mask carved with the bold, swooping curves of the Pacific Northwest tribes. Her eyes sparked with anger.

"Good," she said to Rafe and me as she pulled off the mask. "You're together. I won't have to hunt all over the place to find you." She glanced around the group. "Who else out of this crew is coming?"

Enkou spoke up, gesturing between himself and Hilary. "*Hai,*" Auntie said with a curt nod, and she turned to Kerry and Stoner Boy. "What about you two?"

"Wait. What?" said Jeff. I don't think he'd believed any of it was real until Auntie showed up.

"Just me," said Kerry, as she extricated herself from Jeff's grasp.

I breathed out. The last thing we needed was a clueless human at this gathering. My parents were going to be angry enough. "Webb, you're coming, right?"

Still expressionless, he said, "Wouldn't miss it."

Auntie squinted at him as if attempting to get a fix on him. "This may be a bit tricky," she said. "But I think I can make it work."

"I'll call you later," Kerry said pointedly to Jeff.

"Y-yeah. Yeah. Okay." He backed away and out the door. A few seconds later, I heard the front door shut. I doubted we'd ever see him again.

Kerry looked at me, comprehension dawning in her eyes. Despite her tie to Epona and her friendship with me, her life had been pretty ordinary up to now. I suspected this was the first time a guy she was dating had gotten a full dose of just how abnormal things could get around her.

And then I wondered what Jeff would tell his friends about what had gone on today – and how much of it they would believe.

But there wasn't much time to ponder the ramifications. Auntie put her mask back on, and almost without transition, we were there.

There was a windswept plain, flat as a pancake and featureless as a void. It was surrounded on all sides by distant mountains and lit as if by the sun. But there was no sun. Instead, the sky was filled with millions of stars.

When my mother had talked about this place, she had said each star was a god or goddess. But it was one thing to hear about it, and another thing entirely to see it yourself.

I closed my mouth with an effort.

We had arrived a short distance from the central fire, which burned in a pit in the middle of the plain. I recognized everyone standing next to that fire: my mother and father; Grandfather, in the guise of Blood Clot Boy, the Utes' creation god; White Buffalo Calf Pipe Woman, who had taught the Lakota Sioux how to survive; Epona; Thor and Loki, although I still couldn't think of a good reason for either of Them to be here; Cerridwen, the Celtic goddess of wisdom, who wasn't allied with anybody I knew; and Perun.

Auntie had morphed during the transition. Her mask was no longer a mask, and she seemed to have grown into the pelt. Now, she towered over Rafe, who didn't seem surprised by this turn of events at all. "You could have told me," I hissed at him.

He grinned, his black eyes sparkling. "But this way is more fun!"

I shot him a dirty look as we followed his mother toward the group near the fire.

"Here they are," She said as we advanced. "*You* tell them why they weren't invited."

"Bear Mother," said White Buffalo Calf Pipe Woman, resplendent in glowing white buckskin, "I understand Your love for Your son, and Your faith in him. I love Sage, too, and Webb as well. And I have much faith in them. But Naomi and Joseph believe this is a task for more experienced...."

Auntie threw up one impressively clawed hand. "Save Your breath," She snapped. White Buffalo Calf Pipe Woman drew back as if She'd been slapped. "Naomi and Joseph are human. And while they are certainly experienced, they are too old."

"Now wait just a minute," Mom said, taking a step toward Her.

"Hear me out," said Bear Mother. "Experience grants knowledge, it is true, and the years bring humans much wisdom. But they also teach caution. Tell me, Naomi. Can you envision yourself taking the risks you took twenty years ago?"

"Of course," Mom said, but her voice wasn't as firm as I'd expected it to be.

"And Joseph," Bear Mother said. "You're nearly sixty years old. Are you still as quick as you were back then? Do you still dare to range far to find adventure, or do you stay closer to home?"

Dad gave her a hard look, his eyes glinting amber. But he said nothing.

"When you came to Alaska last week," She continued, "did you fly the whole way, or did you catch a flight?"

"You know I took a plane," he ground out.

"You did?" I said in surprise. I knew it was a long way, but for some reason, I'd assumed he'd flown the whole way himself. His eyes flicked toward me, his gaze apologetic as the amber faded away. It was almost as if I'd caught him out in a lie.

"The torch must be passed to a new generation," Bear Woman proclaimed. "We must meet this bold new threat with boldness. Wisdom is necessary. That is why We are all here. But caution will not do. These are not cautious times.

"The prophecies speak of Buffalo and Coyote no longer. Their time has passed. Now, the prophecies speak of Thunderbird and Raven. You know this. We all know this." She turned to Grandfather. "Do We not, Blood Clot Boy?"

His broad chest, the color of old blood, heaved in a sigh. "I am sorry, Joseph," He said. "But Bear Mother is right. The signs tell Me this is Sage's time." He pointed His chin in my direction. "She and I spoke of it several weeks ago. And I have told you and Naomi this, as well." He gave my father a smile of understanding. "Believe Me, I understand how you feel. I felt the same way when you went haring off on some adventure."

Dad smiled crookedly. "What goes around, comes around, huh?" He looked at Mom. "Honey, we've got to let them go."

Mom crossed her arms and stalked away. Which meant she knew she was beaten.

For a moment, I felt elated. I'd won! They were really going to let me do this my way! They were really going to treat me like an adult, instead of like a dumb kid! I exchanged a stupid grin and a fist bump with Rafe.

But the feeling lasted only for a moment – until the weight of it came crashing down on me. This wasn't playtime. We were really going to have to stop Veles. We were going to have to make Him release the water He had stolen from the Earth – and we were going to have to figure out a way to get Him to give it up without rebooting the whole planet.

Sage the Savior, meet your destiny.

"Shit," I said under my breath.

Mom must have caught my dismay. "Okay, then," she said, not quite snarling. "You're in charge, Sage. What are you going to do?"

"Naomi," Dad said.

"No," she shot back at him. "She's the big kahuna now. She's the Mighty Favog. She needs to give us our marching orders."

I crossed my arms over my midsection and held on, speechless, as if her words had disemboweled me.

I had thought I lived in a close, loving family. I had thought I was lucky. But I was learning that my parents were real people. People with failings. People who could be jealous of their children. People with feet of clay.

"Naomi," Dad said again. His hands were fisted at his sides, and his eyes had turned amber, as if Coyote were about to take over whether he wanted Him to or not. Mom stood apart from him, emitting a cold argent glow so fierce that it eclipsed even White Buffalo Calf Pipe Woman's.

We might have stood that way forever, locked away from each other. But then Webb caught my hand and towed me over to Mom. "Group hug!" he said, as he threw his arms around her shoulders.

For a second, I thought she was going to yell at him. But then she shut her eyes tightly and clung to him, her cheek against his shoulder. Webb grabbed my hand again and tugged me closer.

"Mom?" I whispered. "I'm sorry."

And then she was hugging both of us, and Dad had joined in. "No, *I'm* sorry," she said into my hair. "I'm so sorry, baby."

"It's okay," I repeated, over and over. I wasn't sure if it was true, but if I kept saying it, maybe it would be.

After another few moments, Mom stepped back. She was calmer now, back in control of herself. She swiped at her eyes with a fist and said, "Well, okay. I guess the team just got a little bigger, that's all."

"That's the spirit," Bear Mother said encouragingly.

"So," said Cerridwen in her Welsh accent. "Now that we have all of that settled, what must we do to defeat this worm?"

"We have been discussing this," said Perun, sweeping one arm toward Thor and Loki. "We believe it would be best if I engaged Veles in battle…."

"No!" said Rafe. "We already talked about this, Perun. That's exactly what He wants you to do. You'd be playing right into His hands."

"Do you have a better idea?" asked Thor. He and Perun could have been brothers, I thought. They looked a lot alike, down to the scary-looking weapons held fast in the belts at their waists, except Thor's hair was blond and Perun's was auburn.

Behind Thor, Loki smirked. "He's a Trickster, brother," He said. "Of course he has a better idea." Loki, I knew, was allied with President Holt. That gave him a fair amount of power in human affairs, and as far as I knew, He had always used that power for the good of humanity. But Mom and Dad never fully trusted Him.

Rafe nodded his thanks to Loki and said, "If we can figure out where Veles is hiding the water, we may be able to steal it back without engaging Him in battle."

"And how do you propose to do that?" asked White Buffalo Calf Pipe Woman. She swept one radiant arm around the assembled company. "None of Us gathered here has any affinity for water. Rain and thunder, yes – Perun and Thor, and even you, Sage, can call those and bend them to your purposes. But a large body of water? None of Us could control one."

"He can," I said, hooking my thumb at Enkou.

The gods burst into laughter. "A kappa?" boomed Perun. "But they're nothing but a nuisance!"

"That's not true!" Hilary had been quiet up until now, standing next to Kerry and watching the proceedings with eyes as big as saucers. But she strode forward and faced off against the gods, her outrage making her seem larger than life. "Kappas can be very helpful. For centuries, they have helped Japanese farmers irrigate their fields. And they taught us how to set broken bones so that they mend straight."

While she spoke, Loki approached Enkou. He spoke a few words in Japanese – I was beginning to think everybody spoke Japanese but me – and bowed low. Enkou murmured something to the Norse god and bowed in turn. The water on top of his head spilled onto the ground in front of him, and he froze.

"And they are easily defeated," said Loki as he straightened.

"You creep!" cried Hilary as she ran to Enkou's side.

"Really, brother," said Thor. "That was uncalled for." With a gesture, He called forth a breeze that caused Enkou to plop back onto his butt, as well as a cloud that hovered just above the kappa's head, filling it again with water. As the cloud dissipated, Enkou got to his feet and shook a webbed fist at Loki, chattering angrily.

"*Gomen,*" Loki said with a rueful laugh. "I suppose I deserved that. But it was just too easy."

"Think about it, though," I said. "If Veles has the same opinion of kappas that You all do, He's not going to take Enkou seriously, either. That gives Enkou an advantage. He might be able to sneak past Him and release the water before Veles realizes He's in trouble."

As the gods digested the suggestion, Rafe said, "Where is Veles most likely hiding the water?"

"In Nav," said Perun instantly. "At the foot of the World Tree."

Thor and Loki nodded to each other. "It would make sense to keep a ready supply of water near the roots of Yggdrasil," said Thor.

"And also," Perun reminded them, "Nav is Veles' home."

"Okay," I said, my gut clenching at the enormity of the task before us. "So what you're saying is that we're going to have to break into Veles' house, find all of the water that was supposed to have fallen on the Earth since the beginning of spring, and steal it out from under His nose." I barked a mirthless laugh. "Piece of cake."

"We'll need to distract Veles," Rafe said. "Someone needs to do something that will lure Him away for long enough that Sage, Enkou, and I can sneak into Nav and find the water."

Perun, Thor, and Loki exchanged a look. "I'm sure the three of Us can come up with something," said Loki.

"I'm in," said Dad, grinning. "It'll be just like old times." His grin faded as he looked at me. "Although maybe I should go with Sage. Just in case."

I opened my mouth to tell him to butt out. But then Mom took his arm. "Joseph," she said, nodding in Rafe's direction, "I think guarding Sage is supposed to be *his* job."

"She is right, grandson," said Blood Clot Boy. "Let the young ones do their part for one another."

That sense of prophecy took hold of me again. I looked at Rafe, who seemed stunned, and put a hand on his shoulder. "Shit just got real," I said in a low voice.

He swallowed audibly. "Yeah," he croaked.

I chuckled. "And here you were gonna break up with me."

"No, I...." He paused. "I just wanted to go slower, that's all." He huffed a laugh. "Guess *that's* off the table."

My heart lifted. But still, I said, "Look, I'm not ready to pick out a china pattern, either. Let's just see where this goes, okay?"

He grinned at me. "Okay."

"Are you two done?" Webb asked, rolling his eyes dramatically.

I leaned past Rafe to glower at him. "What's it to you?"

"I'm coming with you," he said, "and I don't want to have to watch the two of you get all squidgy all the time."

"You *what?*" I said. "Mom! Tell him he can't come!"

"Sorry, granddaughter," said Blood Clot Boy, amused. "You have to take him."

Bear Mother nodded in agreement.

There's that stupid prophecy again. "Okay, fine," I grumbled. Actually, I'd figured all along that he'd be coming with. But I had to put on one last show of childishness for Mom and Dad. Just so they didn't think I was completely grown up.

"So that's you, me, Webb, and Enkou," Rafe said.

"Enkou's not going anywhere without me," said Hilary.

"So much for stealth," I said. Our ninja crew was growing bigger by the minute. "Kerry? You've been awfully quiet. Are you coming?"

"I don't think so," she said, shrinking back a little.

Epona crossed to her. "We will work with White Buffalo Calf Pipe Woman to coordinate everyone's efforts."

"And me," said Bear Mother.

"And me," said Cerridwen. I still couldn't figure out why She was here.

"And me," said Mom, clearly glad to have a role defined at last.

"So," Rafe asked, "is there a map to Nav or something?"

Dad exchanged a look with Grandfather. And just like that, I knew how we were going to have to get there. "Oh, no," I said.

"Oh, yes," said Webb, with a knowing nod.

"Oh, shit," I said.

Of Bear Mother and Cerridwen and Kerry

Webb again. I see Sage just rattled on without bothering to explain certain things, so I guess it's up to me.

For instance: Bear Mother. There's a Tlingit legend about a chief's daughter who said some nasty things about bears within earshot of one. The Bear took on the appearance of a human and lured her away to his cave, where she lived with him for some time, and even bore him children. Eventually her brothers found her, killed her Bear husband, and brought her and her children back to the tribe. The legend goes on to say that Bear Mother brought a lot of knowledge of Bear ways back with her, and that knowledge proved very useful for the tribe's continued existence. But the legend is also a cautionary tale about treating all beings with respect. And good for Auntie for reminding the gods – and my parents – of that.

Now, about Cerridwen: I know why She was there, but I can't tell you the reason. Instead, I'll just tell you about Her. In Welsh mythology, Cerridwen's son, Afagddu, was ugly and not particularly talented, so She made a salmon stew for him and simmered it for a year and a day. The Celts believe salmon is the fish of wisdom, and the idea was that one taste of the stew would give Ugly Boy all the wisdom in the world. Cerridwen entrusted a boy named Gwion with the task of stirring the stew. In the process, three drops of stew flew out of the cauldron and fell on Gwion's thumb. When he put his injured thumb in his mouth, he got all the wisdom that was supposed to go to Afagddu. The goddess found out, and an epic shapeshifting chase began. Gwion finally shifted into a kernel of grain and Cerridwen, as a chicken, gobbled him up. Nine months later, She gave birth to the great Welsh bard Taliesin.

And as for Kerry and the loser she was with.... I don't want to talk about it right now.

Chapter 9

The only thing left to do was to set a date for our water liberation effort. We settled on waiting another two weeks, until mid-October. Rafe and I argued that we were risking the future of Earth by waiting that long, but my parents insisted on the delay. Webb was scheduled to take the ACT in another few days, and Rafe, Hilary, and I all had midterms coming up. Mom and Dad didn't want saving the planet to jeopardize our grades.

Although if we failed – or if Veles got tired of waiting for a response from Perun and just went ahead with rebooting the planet – Webb's ACT score would be the least of our worries. As we argued about it with our elders, I felt like I was negotiating my attendance at a midweek party. However, my parents and Rafe's mom were not to be swayed. And our prophecy experts – Blood Clot Boy and my brother, who was supposed to be on my side, damn it – didn't foresee a down side to waiting. So off we went – *shoo! shoo!* – back to campus, with nothing concrete except a plan to meet again in another few days.

I was fuming. All these years, I'd resisted full participation in what you might call the family business. Now I was ready to go – I had my own team, for gods' sake! – and my parents were telling me to cool my heels for two weeks.

So when everyone deserted Rafe and me – in my room, standing next to my bed – I didn't even notice.

Auntie had brought us back, returning in the process to human-in-costume form. She gave me a hug, which was nice of her. Rafe got a big kiss on the cheek, which he appeared to merely tolerate. If I'd been in a better mood, I would have found the expression on his face hilarious.

Enkou took off as soon as Auntie faded out, and Hilary tore off after him. Kerry excused herself to do damage control on Jeff. And there we were.

"Uh," he said awkwardly.

That brought me back to the moment. I'd like to think I had the grace to blush, but it probably didn't show – I was still pretty red in the face from my parents' latest slight. "Never mind that," I told him brusquely. "We need to get to Golden, and we need to do it now."

"We do? Why?"

"Because I need to know how we're going to reopen the path to the underworld at Grandfather's old camp."

He had only ever heard the official version, of course, so I had to clue him in on what had really happened. Loki – yes, the jerk who had just embarrassed Enkou in front of Their fellow gods – had been obsessed with finding Odin's son Baldur in the underworld and bringing Him back to life. Centuries before, Loki had gone off the deep end and had pulled a malicious trick that caused Baldur's death, and Odin had sentenced Loki to eternal punishment for setting it up. During the negotiations over the Second Coming, my mother managed to convince Odin to release Loki from His sentence. I guess it was a time-off-for-good-behavior kind of thing. Anyway, Loki had been a model member of the Norse pantheon since then. And of course, now He was best buds with the President of the United States – although I don't think many people knew that President Holt consorted with a known Trickster.

But the point is that during His search for Baldur, Loki had figured out that one of the entrances to the underworld was on Ute land, and that my great-grandfather was in charge of guarding it. He tried all sorts of stuff to get to that entrance. Finally, he kidnapped Mom, Dad, and several other people, and frog-marched them through the portal and into the underworld. They managed to escape, but on their way out, an earthquake and fire sealed the entrance behind them.

That's what Webb meant when he said the spirits were gone from the mountain meadow above Grandfather's old home. The portal was closed. There was no way to get to Them any more.

Or so I'd thought. But then I saw Dad and Grandfather exchange that look. Now, I wasn't so sure.

"There's something they're not telling me," I finished. "I want to know what it is. I'm tired of them keeping me in the dark."

Rafe shrugged. "Okay. I'm game, I guess. How are we going to get there?"

I looked at him, incredulous. "Drive, of course. The light rail takes too long."

"We could fly," he said with a smirk.

"It's only a half-hour drive!"

"So it's perfect for flying. And it's such a beautiful day."

I'd been under too much strain already. The wheedling tone in his voice just about set my eyes ablaze. "*You* can fly," I said, snatching my purse and my car keys. "*I'm* driving."

I heard him sigh. "No, that's okay. I'm coming."

Forty minutes' worth of awkward silence later, we were bumping up my parents' driveway. Webb was waiting for us on the front porch. "Took you long enough," he said.

I hooked a thumb at Rafe. "Had to fill him in. Where are they?"

"Can't you hear them?" he asked. And now that he mentioned it, I could hear the raised voices coming from the direction of the kitchen: Mom, Dad, and even Grandfather.

The three of them fell silent when the three of us walked in. The room we called the kitchen was a combination kitchen/dining room/sitting room, with a fireplace in the far corner opposite French doors that led to the patio out back. Grandfather was seated in a rocking chair next to the fireplace. He'd thrown a red-and-black patterned afghan over his shoulders, and it made him look like a grizzled warrior in one of those old sepia-tinted photos. Mom was standing with her back to the sink, and Dad had paused in the act of getting something out of the fridge.

I plopped my purse on top of the island with a flourish and said, "So tell me about this entrance to the underworld. The one that supposedly collapsed behind you when you were fleeing for your lives."

"It did collapse," Dad said.

"Then what was that look about?" I said, gesturing between Dad and Grandfather.

Grandfather sighed. "There is another entrance," he said.

"C'mon, Looks Far," said Uncle George. For the first time, I noticed him in the chair opposite Grandfather next to the hearth. "Tell the girl the truth." He nodded at me. "Hello, Sage, how you doin'? And this must be Rafe." He stood and held out a hand. "George Lofton."

"Hi, Uncle George," I said, and gave him a hug after he finished greeting Rafe. I had a soft spot in my heart for the guy. He wasn't a blood relation, but he and my father had been friends forever, and he had been helping out Grandfather for nearly as long. He and Aunt Shannon had an on-again, off-again relationship. "So you tell me, then, since nobody else is going to."

Uncle George cut a look at Grandfather, who waved at him to go on. "Well, okay. There are a boatload of entrances to the underworld," Uncle George said. "The Utes were in charge of the old Mexica entrance because the Mexica abandoned it when they migrated to Mexico. You'd call 'em Aztecs," he explained to Rafe. "We're related, way back there."

"Anyway," Dad said. He'd retrieved a couple of bottles of beer from the fridge, cracked them open, and handed one to Uncle George.

"Right. I got a little off-track." He nodded his thanks at Dad. "Anyway, the point is that there are a whole bunch of ways to get down there. They're all over the world. And any culture with a World Tree in its mythology has an entrance that will take you to that tree – because it's the same tree, whatever they might call it. Just like Jehovah and Allah and Yahweh are all the same guy. Right, Naomi?" He took a long pull on his beer. "Ah. That hits the spot. Thanks, Joseph."

"Why did Loki pick the Mexica entrance, then?" Rafe asked. "Why didn't he use the Norse entrance?"

"Because Odin had somebody watching it, of course," Uncle George said. "All the entrances are guarded. The gods would be fools to leave them open for just anybody to walk in, don't you think? And I wouldn't call any of Them fools. Crazy, maybe, some of Them, like this Veles character. But fools They ain't." He swigged his beer again. "Anyhow, I figure Loki must have weighed his options and seen how we had just one old man in front of our portal, and thought he'd be the easiest to beat." He grinned at Grandfather. "Course, He didn't know Looks Far."

"He did not," Grandfather said with a smile. "But He learned soon enough."

"So where's the next nearest portal?" I asked.

"Now that's an interesting question," he said. "Because the other thing to keep in mind is that they're not all trees."

"Right," said Webb. "The *axis mundi*. Sometimes it's a tree, sometimes it's a mountain, and sometimes it's a column of smoke." He turned to me. "Grandpa Drew told me once that the Black Hills function as an *axis mundi* for the Lakota. The shamans go there to reach the gods."

I thought of the ring of hills that surrounded the blank plain in the otherworld, and nodded. I could see how it would work. "And it's similar for the Utes, I guess," I said, turning to Grandfather. "That's why our portal was here in the Rockies."

"Right," Uncle George said, as Grandfather nodded. "But the portal doesn't have to be a mountain. Or a tree, either. It could be something else." He nodded toward Rafe. "Like a totem pole."

I turned slowly to him. He was looking out the back windows, all innocence. "So when, exactly, where you going to tell me?"

He focused on me with a sigh. "When the time came," he said. "You're not ready yet."

"What do you *mean*, I'm not ready?" I said. I could feel the fire gathering behind my eyes, and at that moment, it would have suited me fine to crisp him up a bit. "We've got the team! We know what we need to do! Why are we stalling?"

"You can't fly."

"I can *so* fly!" I paced toward the French doors, just to be doing something. "You *know* I can!"

"But you're not confident," he said. "Sage, you've flown exactly twice in your life. Once was an accident, and the other time, I had to trick you into it. You don't know anything about compensating for wind currents, or conserving your energy for long flights, or *any*thing. And I'm sorry, but your landings are a joke."

"He's right," said Dad.

I looked at each of my family members in turn. They all looked sympathetic, but I could tell that they also all agreed with Rafe.

"So all that bullshit about the ACT and midterms was a delaying tactic," I said. "Wasn't it?"

"Not entirely," Mom said with a small smile. "Your father and I do want you to do well in school. But yes, in part, we deliberately sought a delay. We didn't want the gods to know how unprepared you were." She twisted her hands together – something she almost never did. "This is my fault. I should have *pushed* you into flying years ago." Mom's special power, granted to her by White Buffalo Calf Pipe Woman, was to apply a special kind of pressure to get people to do what she wanted them to do. She had hardly ever used it on Webb or me.

"It wouldn't have worked," Dad told her. He crossed to where she was standing and drew her into his arms. "And you know that. You can't *push* someone into doing something they don't want to do, and she had a mental block against flying."

"She had a mental block against the woo-woo, period," Mom said, leaning her head on his shoulder.

"You're not wrong," said Webb.

I glared at him. "Fine," I said. "Then how do you see it all going down, little brother?"

He was silent for a few moments, as if weighing his words. At last, he said, "Come here. I want to show you something." And he led me upstairs to his room.

The house had originally had five bedrooms. But when Webb started working on larger-scale projects, Dad knocked out the wall between his room and the next one, doubling the size of my brother's room and giving him a sort of studio. Dad had also built him a bunch of storage cubbies – larger ones for yarn and fabrics, and smaller ones for knitting needles and crochet hooks. There were the usual guy tools there, too – hammers and screwdrivers and pliers, screws and nails and reels of wire – but Webb used the vast majority of the space for his fiber art.

I saw his new installation as soon as I walked in the door. There was no way to miss it – it was the biggest thing I'd ever seen him attempt. It began right next to his bed, which he'd pushed up against one wall, and stretched around the room in a horseshoe shape. He had built the articulated wire armature first, and was hanging pieces of fabric and worked yarn onto it.

At first, it seemed like a jumble of unrelated bits. But something prompted me to unfocus my eyes and look at it again, and when I did, I sucked in a breath. Because what my brother was building was the story of the gods' campaign to save the Earth.

Here was the land, dry as dust. Here were the people fleeing inland to escape the rising seas. Along the top of the structure was the atmosphere, riddled with holes, yet blocking the heat from escaping from the planet.

Farther along, Webb had depicted my dream of Veles. Somehow, he had captured the landscape I'd seen. There was the dragon, poised to strike – and there I was, my arms transformed into fiery wings, my eyes shooting laser beams as I hovered above the ground.

And here was our meeting with Perun at Kenai Fjords – Dad the puffin, Rafe the Raven, and me again, melting the glacier with the warmth of my feet.

And here was our meeting with the gods earlier in the day.

The next several panels were blank. I turned to Webb. "This is awesome. But why haven't you filled these in yet?"

"I can't see what happens," he said. Because he was involved, of course.

I looked past the bare armature to a spot toward the very end, where the story picked up again. That panel appeared to be complete. He saw where I was looking and said, "You wanted to see how it's all going to go down. That's it. That's the end game."

I was torn. On one hand, I wanted desperately to know that I wasn't going to fuck everything up. And part of me was still stuck in reality mode. I wanted to know whether it would be science or woo-woo that pulled our *cojones* out of the fire at the last.

But on the other hand, what if Webb's vision told me we would fail?

"It's not set in stone, is it?" I said. "Things could change."

"Things can always change," he said.

So even if the end game was a disaster, we could still turn it around. *I* could still turn it around.

And yet.

Would I slack off if I knew we would win, thereby causing us to fail? And if I knew we were destined to fail, would I redouble my efforts to win, or simply give up?

Did it matter either way?

"No," I said at last. "No, that's okay. I don't want to know."

Webb smiled broadly and clapped me on the shoulder. Then he followed me back downstairs, where everyone waited for us. For me.

I looked around at their faces – every one of them dear to me – and said, "Okay. We've got two weeks. Teach me how to fly."

Chapter 10

It was a grueling weekend. Rafe and I returned to Boulder that night to pack and head back to my parents' place. Then, bright and early Saturday morning, the lessons began.

I learned very quickly just how much I didn't know. Dad and Rafe were patient, as far as it went. But they would go off on these esoteric discussions about aerodynamics and so on. I understood the physics behind what they were talking about, but some of their conversations were even above *my* head.

And the two of them were not above tweaking me. At one point, Dad led me far into a cave. It was a long flight – so long that I was half-sure we were going to fly all the way through the Rockies and end up on the Western Slope. But we also made a bunch of turns. I knew I had no hope of memorizing the route, so I stopped paying attention to the doglegs and switchbacks, and simply followed him. Then suddenly, he dropped from the air and turned into a bug, leaving me to find my own way back out. It took me most of Sunday – only to discover my father waiting for me. He had taken a side tunnel with a much more straightforward route back. "Feel for the freshest air," he said, as I fumed silently at him. "And always look for the quickest way out. It may not be the way you came in."

Rafe's tricks were of another sort. I soon learned his Raven was easily distractible. We'd be flying along, discussing something or other, and suddenly he'd see something shiny and he'd be gone. Usually the thing that caught his eye was nothing – trash, maybe, or a brightly-dressed runner in the National Forest. Sometimes, he would follow a wolf to the site of a recent kill. And sometimes the wolves would follow him, thinking he would lead them to their next meal. Although my presence seemed to put them off.

They're not used to seeing a flaming bird, he said with a smirk.

I was also learning more about my parents' ability to talk mind-to-mind. Rafe and I had naturally fallen into it from the first, but Mom had had to struggle to converse with Dad when he was in a non-human form. And she couldn't figure out how to mind-speak with me at all. I considered it a blessing in disguise. I didn't really want to know what my mother was thinking most of the time, and I didn't exactly welcome Mom knowing my secret thoughts, either. Particularly when most of my secret thoughts revolved around Rafe.

Luckily, mind-reading wasn't a component of the ability I shared with Rafe. Or at least, I couldn't read *his* thoughts. He had to form them into words and aim them at me before I could understand them. And if he knew what *I* was thinking, he never let on. And I'm pretty sure he would have reacted to at least some of my thoughts, if only by blushing.

In any case, we didn't have much time for the pursuit of those thoughts. Between flying lessons and homework, I barely had time to go to the bathroom.

On Sunday night, we faced a decision: drive back to campus, or spend the next two weeks commuting? Flying lessons were easier in Golden – there weren't as many potential spectators in my parents' neighborhood – and the drive wasn't impossible to do on a daily basis. On the other hand, learning to fly was exhausting, and I wasn't crazy about adding a commute of an hour and change to my daily schedule. I was tempted to just skip class for the next two weeks. Rafe, however, wasn't willing to take that much of a risk with his grades.

"But don't make your decision based on what I need," he said as we sat on my parents' patio, enjoying a fire in the fire pit and holding hands in the gathering dark. "You don't have to drive me back and forth. I'm perfectly capable of flying."

"So am I," I said, more confidently than I felt. "How come you don't have your own car, anyway?"

"I gave it away."

"You what?"

"It's a cultural thing," he said. "You've heard of a potlatch?"

"Of course." I knew that in some Native cultures, people would celebrate their good fortune by feeding the whole community and giving everything they owned away. They would get it all back eventually – if not the precise thing they gave away, then something that would serve the same purpose. "The Lakota do something similar."

"Okay. Well, when I got accepted to CU, Mom threw a potlatch and I gave away everything I owned. Including my car."

I had only caught a glimpse of his room when we stayed at his house, and I remembered thinking that it was pretty spartan. But it had never occurred to me that he had once had more than that. And then I thought of my own room in the house behind us, chockablock with all my childhood dolls and toys. "Was it hard to give it all up?" I asked.

"Actually," he said with a grin, "it made it a lot easier to pack for college." His smile faded. "There were a couple of things I wish I could have kept, though."

"Like what?"

"Stupid stuff." He shook his head. "Mostly things that reminded me of my father."

"Where is he, anyhow? You never talk about him."

Silently, he poked at the fire. The day had been warm for late September, and we'd needed only light jackets when we came outside, but the temperature was dropping rapidly. I wondered whether it would snow tonight. And then I shook my head. It wasn't going to snow – not with Veles capturing all of the precipitation.

"What?" he said, catching my expression.

I shrugged. "Just wondering if it will ever snow again."

He nodded and lapsed back into silence.

I gave him a moment, and then said, "So about your father."

"Oh, right." He dropped the poker but stayed hunched forward in his chair. "I told you that he works for an oil extraction company. He was transferred to their facility in Barrow when I was a little kid." In the firelight, his eyes seemed to have nothing but depth. "I used to spend summers with him, but then Mom and he had a falling out over something that happened while I was up there, and I never went back. I haven't seen him now in…." He paused. "Wow. Five years. A quarter of my life."

I put a hand on his shoulder. "That's got to be hard. I'm sorry."

His glance shied away from me. "It happens." He looked down at his knees for a moment. Then he looked up at me. "So," he said, and stopped. He reached one hand out and cupped my cheek, stroking my face with his thumb. Then he kissed me.

Somehow, we ended up entwined in each other's arms.

Behind us, my mother cleared her throat, and we sprang apart. "I'm sorry to interrupt," she said with the tiniest trace of a grin. "But were you planning to stay the night again? It's no trouble. I was just wondering."

"Actually," I said, trading a smile with Rafe, "we were just discussing that."

Mom played along. "And had you decided?"

"I think we should go back," he said.

His decisiveness caught me by surprise. But when we got back to Boulder, I discovered that he had no intention of going back to his room in the dorm. And at my place, there was no one to interrupt us.

I knew I should have paid more attention to Jeff.

"Have you guys seen this?" asked Kerry as Rafe and I emerged from my room the next morning.

"Good morning to you, too," I said. "We have coffee, don't we?" I went into the kitchen to make myself a cup. "Rafe, there's hot water for tea, if you want some."

"Shit," he said in reply. Although not in reply to *me*.

I left the coffee machine to do its thing and joined him and Kerry in the living room. They were staring at the *CU Independent* on Kerry's tablet. More precisely, they were staring at the photo at the top of the paper's web page. It was a shot of the interior of my room from near the door. There I was – or at least, there was the back of my head. And Rafe's, and Hilary's. He'd gotten a decent profile shot of Enkou. And Webb's hologram was looking right at the camera.

"Shit," I echoed. "Why didn't Webb say something to us? Come to that," I said to Kerry, "why didn't you tell him to put his phone away?"

"I thought he was checking the time!" She looked at the photo again. "When I get my hands on that bastard...."

Someone knocked at the door. The three of us exchanged guilty looks – although what we had to be guilty about, I couldn't have told you. It's not like we were harboring Enkou or anything. As far as I knew.

"Is Hilary here?" I asked.

"I don't know. I think she might have an early class on Mondays."

"You go check her room. I'll answer the door."

Kerry nodded and headed down the hall. I took two steps toward the door and looked down. "Shit," I said again. I was wearing my sleep tee, and Rafe was similarly dressed. Maybe I could get them to go away without letting them in.

Whoever they were, they knocked again. I sighed and went to open the door a crack. "Hi," I said, making a show of blinking at the light. "Sorry – I just got up. Is there something I can help you with?"

"Campus security," said the uniformed man who stood on our stoop. He flashed a wallet that contained something that may or may not have been a legit ID. "May I come in?"

"Sorry," I repeated. "I don't think so. I really did just get up." And it hadn't escaped my notice that he hadn't mentioned a search warrant.

He regarded me silently for a moment. Then he said, "Does Hotaru Takahashi live here?" He had to consult the tablet he was holding for the name.

I blinked. "We have a roommate whose last name is Takahashi, but her first name is Hilary." As I said it, I flashed on a memory of Enkou calling her *Hotaru-chan*. I hoped my dawning recognition didn't show on my face.

"That's her," he said. "I'd like to speak with her."

"I don't know if she's here," I said. "She keeps kind of odd hours."

"Would you check for me, please?"

"Um, sure. Hang on." And I shut the door in his face. I turned away to behold a beaming Kerry coming back up the hall. From behind her came the sound of the back door snicking shut.

I shot Kerry a thumbs-up and opened the door again, rubbing my eyes with one hand for effect. "Yeah, no, sorry," I said. Then I saw the empty porch. "Shit." I shut the door. "He must have heard her leave. We need to...."

Rafe held my mug of coffee out to me. "We need to do what? There isn't anything we can do." He shrugged. "The cops will question Hilary or not. They'll find Enkou or not."

"And if they detain him," I said, "how will we take him with us to the underworld?"

That made him pause – but only for a moment. "Drink your coffee. We'll figure something out."

Our brilliant plan did not bode well for our ability to outwit Veles.

It turned out the campus cops were smarter than we'd always given them credit for. While Cop Number One was knocking on our front door, Cop Number Two had staked out the back door. There was no way Hilary could have avoided him, short of barricading herself in the house and yelling, "You'll never take me alive, coppers!" through her window.

Or calling on one of the gods to get her out of there, I guess. But none of us thought of that until much later.

In any case, the cops got her. And they persuaded her to take them to where Enkou was hiding in Boulder Creek, and picked him up, too. By the time we caught up with them, both Hilary and the kappa were cooling their heels in a locked room at the campus security office while the cops talked with Boulder police about pressing charges.

I don't know why it didn't occur to me until that moment to call my mother, the lawyer.

"Hi, Sage," she said "Did you forget something?"

I paused for a second, wondering whether I *had* forgotten something last night. Rafe and I had been in somewhat of a fever to get on the road, after all. But then I realized Mom was just asking me for the reason for my call. "Um, no. That's not.... Listen, Hilary's in a bit of a jam." And I explained – succinctly, I thought – our predicament.

Mom sighed. "See if you can stall them for half an hour."

"Thanks, Mom. We really appreciate it." But she'd already hung up.

True to her word, Mom arrived just a hair over thirty minutes later, with Dad riding shotgun. He hung out with Kerry, Rafe, and me while Mom went to work on the cops.

Ten minutes after their arrival, Hilary and Enkou walked free, with Mom behind them. As Kerry produced a cucumber from her backpack – thereby earning Enkou's undying gratitude – Dad asked Mom in a low voice, "What did you plead, counselor?"

"Lack of jurisdiction and diplomatic immunity," she told him in the same quiet tone.

I grinned at her as we emerged into the sunshine. "You made that up," I said.

"I did not. The courts have never really settled the issue of jurisdiction over the gods," she said. "While even President Holt could be tried and convicted in a U.S. court...."

"Not a bad idea," Dad said under his breath.

"I heard that," Mom said, and he flashed her a Coyote grin. "Anyway," she resumed, "the point is that the gods are not American citizens. And while we have what you might call diplomatic relations with Them, it's not like we've signed any sort of treaty." She snorted.

"We were lucky to get the Second Coming accord. Which, by the way, is not in writing.

"In any case, Their position is that *They* have jurisdiction over *us*, not the other way around."

"So the gods can't be thrown in jail?" Rafe said. "Interesting."

"That was my argument to the police, yes," Mom said. Then she pitched her voice to carry to the front of the group. "But that doesn't mean They can violate the law. They have to be model citizens."

Hilary glanced back, looking chastened. The experience with the cops had apparently made an impression on her. Figuratively speaking, the jury was still out on Enkou. Hilary whispered something to him – presumably translating my mother's words – and the kappa waved in acknowledgement without turning around. Mom's mouth set in an expression I was all too familiar with.

Dad saw it, too. "Is it too early for lunch?" he asked, in an effort to lighten the mood.

"I have class," said Kerry regretfully. "I'll see everyone later." And she took off toward the psych building.

At the word *class*, Rafe and I exchanged a guilty look, and pulled out our phones at the same time. "Crap," he said. "We're missing Water Chem."

"Correction: we've missed Water Chem." I grinned at my father. "So we have plenty of time for lunch. Thanks, Dad."

Hilary also begged off – something about restaurants not being kappa-friendly. So it was just Mom, Dad, Rafe, and me for lunch.

"Webb's gonna be jealous that we got Thai without him," I said with a sisterly smirk.

Mom and Dad traded a look. "It was nice to see Kerry this morning," Mom said. "How's she doing?"

I shrugged. "Fine, I guess. Same as always. You know Kerry."

"Is she seeing anyone?"

Ah. Now I knew what this was about. "Webb's been moping, hasn't he?" I asked.

"He hasn't been himself since you guys all Skyped the other day," she said.

"I didn't notice anything weird over the weekend," I said. "Although I was so busy that I barely saw him."

The food arrived just then, and I waited until our server left before going on. "To answer your question, yes, she's been seeing someone – the idiot who took the photo that got Hilary in trouble this morning." I rolled my eyes. "I assume that's over now. I *hope* it's over, anyway, after this. I hope she has the sense to break up with him." I shook my head over my pad Thai. "I don't know what she ever saw in him in the first place. I thought he was a loser from the get-go. But please don't tell Webb I said that." I looked up at my parents. "He'll try to make a play for her, and he's just going to end up embarrassing himself."

"Webb has a crush on Kerry?" asked Rafe.

"Oh, man," I said. "It's more than a crush. It's been going on forever. I keep trying to get her to talk to him – you know, to let him down easy – but she hasn't done it."

"Maybe I should talk to her," Mom said. My eyebrows went up, and so did Dad's. "Oh, come on, you two," Mom said. "I wouldn't try to *push* her."

"I really think this is ought to be between Webb and Kerry," I said. Ruefully, I muttered, "I just wish she'd do it already."

Chapter 11

The next two weeks passed in a blur. I kept up with my homework – barely – but I hoped like hell that we didn't cover anything too important in class. I was grateful for our outdoor labwork in Water Chem, though – the chilly temperature helped me to stay awake.

I dragged my ass out of bed that Saturday morning for my final day of flight training – or, as I had privately dubbed it, Flying Boot Camp – and met Dad and Rafe in backyard. To my surprise, Grandfather was there, too. He was seated in a chair next to the unlit fire pit, a blanket wrapped around his shoulders against the chill.

I gave him a hug. "Want me to light a fire for you?"

But he shook his head. "Your mother is bringing me something hot to drink. I will be fine. I'm here to see what you've got." He sat back and regarded me with a gimlet eye, his arms crossed under the blanket.

I grinned. "You think an audience is gonna scare me? You just wait. I'm gonna fly circles around these guys." I hugged him again and trotted over to where my father and Rafe were waiting. "Let's do it," I said.

"We're doing something different today," said Dad. And almost without transition, we were in the gods' world.

I spun slowly, taking in the nothingness. Apart from the four of us – Grandfather had made the transition, too, and sat cross-legged on the ground a short distance away – there was nothing here at all. The bleak plain seemed to go for miles in every direction, with neither flora nor fauna to break the monotony. Even the ceremonial fire pit was gone.

"Why are we here?" I asked. "Is there a meeting today or something?"

"No," Dad said. "We're here for a different reason. You and Rafe will probably meet Veles in the Underworld, which is an extension of this world. And things work a little differently here. So I want the two of you to work on your flying here – just so you can get a feel for what it will be like."

I nodded. "Makes sense." I looked at Rafe for corroboration....

…and in the time it took for me to turn my head, I was alone in a jungle.

I whipped my head from side to side. "Dad? Rafe? Where are you guys?"

In answer, a little green snake slithered over my foot.

I pulled back with a hiss. "Not funny, Dad," I said to the snake. But it just kept moving away, and I shivered. It had been a real snake. This was a real jungle. And I didn't know either how I'd gotten here or how to get home.

I am not usually prone to panic, but at that moment, I was pretty close to gibbering.

And then I remembered that I was supposed to be practicing my flying. *Well, fine. Suck it up, Sage. Maybe flying is the ticket out of here.* I shifted and launched myself toward the treetops.

It was a long way up, but at last I cleared the trees. And then I began to panic again, because the jungle seemed to spread out in every direction. I couldn't even tell where I had broken through the canopy; every treetop looked just like every other treetop. I hovered miserably in midair and thought, *I just want to go home.*

As soon as I formulated the words, I nearly flew into the side of a mountain. I banked, and looked at the snow-capped peaks surrounding me. If this wasn't home, it was a pretty good imitation. There were Long's Peak and Mt. Elbert – the mountains I grew up with. I greeted them as if they were old friends, and then set a course for our house.

But I couldn't find it. Oh, I found the spot where it was supposed to be. But the house wasn't there. Neither was the town of Golden. Or Boulder. Or, for that matter, Denver.

Even though it looked like I was in Colorado – *my* Colorado – I was still in the otherworld.

And as soon as I came to that realization, the landscape morphed yet again.

The mountains below me were now blue with ancient glaciers. I recognized them. The last time I'd been here had been in a dream, and Veles had slithered out from behind the very rock ahead of me.

Oh no, I thought, and tried to back away. Except I forgot I was flying. I missed my rhythm and began flailing in midair.

As I fought to recover my equilibrium, something big and sinuous flashed past me overhead. "So, little firebird," it purred, "we meet again." The creature pulled up in the air just a few yards away from me. "You don't look so tough now. I bet I could take you out with a single breath." And as I watched in horror, too disoriented to react, Veles pulled in a big breath of air. I shut my eyes against the fiery blast that was sure to end my life.

But it didn't come. Instead, the god laughed at me.

"Oh, come now," He said, still chuckling. "That would be too easy. And anyway, I need for you to survive."

Leave her alone! From out of nowhere, a streak of ebony crossed in front of me and began flying around the god's head, harrying Him. Distracting Him from attacking me.

Rafe! I cried. *Be careful!*

Get out of here, Sage! he yelled.

I was aghast. If I did, he would be toast. *I can't leave you!*

Go on!

No! Seeing Rafe in danger was all I needed to pull myself together. I concentrated my anger right behind my eyes, and let loose. It was a foolhardy thing to do with Rafe in the vicinity. I could have as easily struck him as Veles, as erratic as his flight path was. But luck or the gods were with me, and I scored a direct hit on the dragon's nose.

Veles let loose with a roar of frustration and pain.

Come on! Rafe cried as he darted past me. He didn't need to tell me twice. I executed a somersault and streaked away from Veles, trusting that Rafe could lead us both out of danger.

But even as the mountains below us turned friendlier and more familiar, I could hear the dragon's calm, calculating voice in my head. "So. The little firebird has a soft spot. I can use that."

I thought I was scared before, but that was nothing. I realized that I had just made a big mistake. Before, I had been the only one in Veles's crosshairs. Now He knew about Rafe – and Veles had said nothing about needing to keep *him* alive.

With Rafe along, finding home was easy. All I did was follow him, and all of a sudden, we were there. And we had a welcoming committee: not just Dad and Grandfather, but Mom and Webb were there to watch us land and shift back to human form.

"Where did you go?" Dad asked, grabbing us both by an elbow. "I lost you."

"Veles," said Rafe, out of breath.

"*Shit.*" Dad pulled me into a hug. "What happened?"

"He came out of nowhere," I said, trying not to hyperventilate. "One minute, I was flying above the Front Range, and the next minute I was back in those mountains I dreamed about, and Veles was getting ready to attack me."

"It looked like Alaska to me," said Rafe.

Dad shook his head. "It's the otherworld. It could have been anywhere, or nowhere."

The adrenaline surge was draining out of me. Suddenly exhausted, I took a seat on a bench near the fire pit with a *whoof*. Rafe joined me, lacing his fingers through mine. "You can't go back there," I told him.

He laughed in disbelief. "What? What are you talking about?"

I shook my head. "He knows about you now."

"And?"

My fear was rising again. I forced myself to take a couple of calming breaths before I spoke. "How does Veles always initiate His fights with Perun? He steals something Perun values." I looked around at the faces of my family with a growing sense of horror. "All of you are in danger. Oh, gods. I wish I'd never agreed to do this." I disentangled my hand from Rafe's and hugged myself.

What the hell had I been thinking? After all the years I'd spent refusing to take part in the family business, I'd allowed myself to get sucked into this crazy scheme, and now the lives of everyone I loved were at risk. I should have resisted the siren song of magical flight. I should have stuck to my guns. And especially, I should never have gotten involved with Rafe. My family was one thing – Mom and Dad had been through this before. But Rafe didn't grow up with our crazy history. He didn't deserve this. He didn't deserve any of it.

"I can't do it," I said. "I quit." And I fled into the house and barricaded myself in my room. I lay down facing the far wall and stared at nothing, with a pillow clutched to my middle, as if that simple action could keep everything in my life from falling apart.

I don't know how long I lay there for sure. But it was Webb who eventually came after me. He let himself in quietly and sat on the edge of my bed. He didn't try to touch me, which was a smart move on his part. All he did was ask quietly, "Do you want to know what happens?"

I remembered the project in his room. "No."

"Okay." He sighed and got up.

"Wait." I rolled partway over, loosening my death grip on the pillow. "Wait."

He paused, and I had the irrational thought that I ought to commit this moment to memory. For my brother didn't look like a kid any more. He held himself gravely, his stance almost fatalistic. As if he knew I was going to change my mind, and how important it would be.

I suppose he did, at that.

At last, I asked, "Will we win?"

What I really wanted to know was whether we would all survive. But I was afraid to hear the answer – and anyway, survival was a complicated thing. We could live, but still be changed forever, and not necessarily in a good way. But if we saved the world in the end, then whatever sacrifices we would make might be worth it.

His smile was tinged with sadness. "Yes," he said. "Yes, we'll win." And moved toward the door.

"Webb?"

One hand on the doorknob, he turned back and waited.

"Is there any other way?" Some miracle, maybe? Some divine last-minute reprieve?

"No," he said, and let himself out.

I lay there for another few moments with my eyes closed. Then I cast aside the pillow and swung my legs over the side of the bed. I took a moment to scrub my face with my hands, and then I stood.

My future had never looked bleaker. But there was only one way to get through it.

I went back outside. Mom, Dad, and Rafe had taken seats around the fire pit, and were speaking with Grandfather in low, urgent tones.

Rafe spotted me first. He fell silent and sat back, his expression impassive. One by one, they turned to me. Dad looked worried and Mom looked as if she was restraining herself from hopping up to hug me. Only Grandfather looked serene.

"You knew all along, didn't you?" I said to him. "Just like Webb. You knew I couldn't quit."

"I knew you *wouldn't* quit," he said.

I nodded in acknowledgement of the difference. Then I shoved my hands in the kangaroo pocket of my sweatshirt and stared at the ground. "So I guess it doesn't matter at this point. Veles already knows who I am, and He already knows who all of you are. And He seems bound and determined to get me to fight Him." I snorted mirthlessly. "Even if I tried to quit, He wouldn't let me. He'd probably track me down and make me fight. He'd...." A lump had formed in my throat. I had to stop for a moment to clear it. "He'd come after each of you, one at a time, until I couldn't take it any more." I looked up. "I'm really starting to hate that guy."

"Good," Dad said.

"He is not evil," Grandfather said. "Remember that. He is acting in His own self-interest, yes. But He is only doing what He thinks is best."

Mom huffed a laugh. "Even if it means destroying the Earth."

"Destruction and rebirth." Perun appeared behind Rafe. He walked – or maybe glided is a better description of His movement – anyway, He took up a post between Rafe and Grandfather. "This is the only way He knows to make the world right again." The Slavic thunder god regarded me with an apology in His eyes. "And He is only targeting you because He sees Me in you," He said.

I nodded again. I hadn't made the connection consciously, but I'd known it all along. Perun and I were both Thunder Beings, after all. I crossed to the fire pit and crouched beside Mom's chair. "So what do we do?"

Webb came out the back door in time to hear my question. "We go through the gate and find the water Veles is hiding, and get it back," he said as he joined us.

I cast him a sidelong glance. "It sounds so simple when you say it like that." Maybe it was the gleam that never left his eye, but I had to go on. "You got a plan?"

He picked it up and ran with it. "Yeah, I've got a plan," he said, in a tone that meant, *I can't believe you just asked me that.*

"How much of a plan?" Rafe challenged him.

"How much of a plan, he asks," Webb scoffed. He paused. "Twelve percent."

"*Twelve percent* of a plan?" Rafe cried.

"Better than eleven percent," said Dad, stifling a grin.

Rafe, still straight-faced, slashed one hand in his direction. "You keep out of this," he growled. "Twelve percent is not a plan."

"It's barely a concept," I muttered, but I couldn't suppress a giggle any longer.

The four of us dissolved in laughter. Grandfather rolled his eyes up to look at Perun, who was regarding us with a bemused expression.

Mom nodded and said with heavy sarcasm, "Hilarious. You're all hilarious." But I could tell she wanted to grin, too.

"So where is this gate, anyway?" I said when my giggles had subsided. "How do we get there?"

Rafe's mischievous smile had not yet faded. "We have to fly."

I groaned. "Somehow," I said, "I knew you were going to say that."

Chapter 12

In the end, we all flew hypersonic coach: Mom and Dad, Webb and Hilary, and Rafe and me. Webb insisted on coming along. He said he had to be there, but he wouldn't tell us why. Hilary came because Rafe said we might need Enkou, and the kappa wasn't about to go anywhere without her. Mom, Dad, and Auntie were to be our anchors in this world – just in case we needed help getting back.

Nobody had suggested that Grandfather come along, and the old man seemed content to stay behind. I think we all recognized that his days of battling the gods were behind him. I did prevail upon Kerry to drive up from Boulder to stay with him while we were gone. She wouldn't be much help if something went wrong in the otherworld, but Epona could be. And it was certainly possible that Grandfather would need help in *this* world while we were gone.

I waved goodbye to Kerry – she and Webb were in the kitchen, and she was laughing at something my brother had just said – and ran smack into Aunt Shannon as I crossed the living room to the front door. She had decided to stay with Kerry and Grandfather in case, she said, they both needed help.

Aunt Shannon didn't look like Kerry at all. She was taller than Mom, although not as tall as me, and she had fading auburn curls. Although if she and Kerry stood side by side, it was obvious they were related.

She gave me a big hug. Then, always the counselor, she looked carefully at my face. "Are you okay?" she asked. "Do you think you're ready for this?"

I snorted. "Hell, no, I'm not ready. None of us is ready except Perun."

"But Veles isn't after Perun."

"I know." I regarded her steadily.

Her mouth twisted. "You are so much like your mother. It's okay to be scared, you know. I spent *months* being scared shitless for your parents."

"You did it so they didn't have to," I said, grinning. It was an old joke.

"No, I did it because neither one of them would admit to it." Aunt Shannon shook her head. "I just couldn't get over it. Your mother would just forge ahead and forge ahead. She'd have, like, a split second of doubt, and then...." She did jazz hands as her face split in a smile. "All better! And she'd be off to the races again." She snorted at a memory. "That's why she dated Brock for so long. She just never gave herself more than a minute to think about it."

"Brock who?"

She looked at me in surprise. "Brock Holt. You know, President Holt?"

I blinked. "Mom dated President Holt?"

"Oh, my God, yes. For *years*. Your mother never told you?"

"No. Is that why Dad doesn't like him?"

"That's one of several reasons," Mom said as she joined us. "Thanks for giving away *that* family secret, Shannon."

"Oh, come on, Naomi. It's time the kids knew." She seemed to imply that there was more we hadn't been told.

"Yeah, Mom," I said. "It's time we knew. What else have you been keeping from us?"

She cut a withering glance at Aunt Shannon and said to me, "We'll discuss it later. Is your luggage in the car?"

"Of course."

"Then let's get moving or we'll miss our flight."

I turned back to Aunt Shannon, who enveloped me in another hug. "We'll talk later," she whispered in my ear, and kissed my cheek. I shot her a surreptitious thumbs-up and went to get in the car.

Our family owned quite a fleet. Besides the cars Webb and I drove, we had Dad's work truck, a beat-up SUV that Mom called our urban assault vehicle, and the hovercar she had insisted we buy as soon as they were available.

"It's a toy, Naomi," Dad had said. "And a hellaciously expensive toy, at that."

"I don't care. I want my flying car," she'd said. "Dick Tracy said we'd have them by the year 2000. That was twenty-five years ago, Joseph. I'm not waiting any longer."

"Who's Dick Tracy?" Webb had asked, but didn't get an answer. We had to do a web search, and even then, the answer made no sense to us – some cartoon cop had promised Mom a flying car?

It must have made sense to Dad, though, because a couple of weeks later, we had a hovercar. It was tiny – the first ones were all two-seaters – and so mostly, it just sat in the driveway. Mom talked about trading it in for a newer, roomier model, but she never quite got around to it. So we had to take the SUV to the airport.

Mom was already in the driver's seat by the time I got outside. "There's Sage," said Dad as I climbed in behind the shotgun seat and next to Rafe. "Now where's Webb?" He rolled down his window and yelled, "Hey, Webster! Let's go!"

"I'll go get him," Mom said, unbuckling her seat belt.

But before she could open her door, Webb emerged from the house with his shoulders hunched. "Come on, son," Dad said unnecessarily, as Webb climbed in behind Rafe and me, and slammed the door behind him.

"Let's get the fuck out of here," he growled, looking pointedly away from the house.

"Andrew Joseph!" Mom said, using both of his real names – never a good sign.

Apparently I was the only one who'd been at the right angle to get a glimpse of his face as he got in. He had looked to be on the verge of tears, and I had a pretty good idea why – although I could have kicked Kerry's ass for her lousy timing. "Leave him alone," I told Mom.

She must have caught the message I was telegraphing her with my gaze, because she turned around and started the engine without another word.

I gripped Rafe's hand and hoped the rocky beginning wasn't an omen for the rest of our trip.

Auntie picked us up in Anchorage. "Long flight, huh? You all look exhausted. Rafe, give me a hand with their bags."

"We've got 'em," Dad said, elbowing Webb. My brother's mood hadn't improved, but he trudged ahead of Dad and Rafe toward the luggage carousel.

Auntie raised an eyebrow at the men's retreating backs, but turned to us with a smile. "Well, I'm glad everyone arrived safely, anyway. Hello, Hotaru. Enkou speaks very highly of you."

"He made it, then?" Hilary asked in relief. I was relieved, too. I'd been wondering how Enkou was going to get here, since he didn't come on the plane with us. Of course, that would have been awkward. It's not like a three-foot-tall ninja turtle would have a passport.

"Oh, yes, he's been here for a couple of hours. Don't worry – I'm well-stocked with cucumbers."

As we left the terminal for Auntie's car, bundling up against the cold, I leaned over to Hilary. "So your real name is Hotaru?"

"Yeah," she said. "But I've been going by Hilary since grade school. It's easier for Americans to say." *Ah've bin goin'. Eeziah tuh say.*

Mentally, I slapped myself. Maybe it was the stress, I thought, that had caused me to fall back into the habit of mocking Hilary's speech in my head. But I knew I couldn't afford to do it any more. We needed her. Besides, I liked her. And it wasn't going to get any less stressful from here on out.

It almost seemed as if Auntie's house would expand to fit whatever size crowd was coming to stay. I bunked that night with Hilary in the same room where I'd slept before. Then, it had had just one twin bed, but a second had materialized in the interim. Webb slept on the floor in Rafe's room, and Mom and Dad took yet another bedroom that I hadn't noticed the last time I was here.

As I got ready for bed, I pulled my dream helmet from my overnight bag. Then I glanced over my shoulder at Hilary and put it away again.

I'd never before had a roommate who I didn't feel completely comfortable with – or at least, not since I'd begun wearing Webb's woven scraps of yarn to bed every night. I'd felt weird about it when Rafe stayed over, but as soon as I told him what it was for, he insisted that I wear it. "I don't even know if there's any magic in it," I'd said as I pulled it on. "It might work on the power of suggestion."

"I would believe that if Veles hadn't found you on the one night you weren't wearing it," he'd said. "Let's not take any chances."

Those words of Rafe's echoed in my head as I stowed the dream helmet away again. I was sure I could tell Hilary without her looking at me funny. I mean, if anybody was going to cut me slack for having a dream helmet, it would have to be the girl who was prepared at all times to provide water and cucumbers to a kappa. And yet I just didn't want to get into it with her.

Needless to say, I should have just gotten into it with her.

I looked out an airplane window at the frozen ground below me. It was the same view I'd had earlier in the day, flying into the airport in Anchorage.

Then I looked around and realized the plane was gone.

Then I noticed the landscape had changed.

What was really weird was that I knew I was dreaming. But I couldn't wake myself up. It was as if the gods had ordained that I was to have this dream, and there was nothing I could do to stop it. I moaned, but kept flying. I figured the way to end this creeping sense of dread I was feeling was to just have the damn dream already. So I ignored my fears and flew on.

Maybe I was more like my mother than I knew.

Before long, the now-familiar snowcapped peaks appeared ahead of me. The region looked even more desolate than it had the last time I'd been here — or maybe I was simply paying attention to it this time, for once. The last couple of times, I'd been in self-preservation mode, too shocked by being here at all to do anything but react.

I scanned the ground and shook my flaming head. No, it was definitely more barren. In fact, it almost looked…charred. Had I done that with my eyes when I attacked Veles? Had I flown too close to the ground? Or had the dragon Himself taken out His frustration and anger on the very Earth?

"Ah," the dragon said, sounding so close that I jumped. "The little firebird is back. Good." The dragon nosed His way out from behind a distant peak and made His way toward me, His body undulating in the air as if He were swimming through it.

I stanched my fear and forced myself to take a good, hard look at Him. He had a thin, pointed snout, unlike those of Chinese dragons that were said to be friendly, and iridescent scales that seemed to change color every time he moved. He had neither hands nor feet, although vestigial flippers were positioned on either side of His ruff and appeared to help steer Him through the air. Clearly He could hear, although I saw nothing on His head that looked like an ear. Maybe He heard with something like gills. Maybe He strained the air for sound, the way whales strained water through their teeth for sustenance.

"Look, Veles," I said. I should have been surprised to find that I had the power of audible speech in this dream world, but I wasn't. "I don't know why You're so intent on riling me up. I've got no argument with You."

"Oh, but you do, little firebird," He purred. "For you believe yourself capable of fixing this planet." He made a low, rumbling sound that I realized was supposed to be laughter. "You? Pathetically small and woefully unprepared as you are? Anyone with sense can see that you have no hope of saving this world." Those mountains must have been a really long way away — He had not yet closed half the distance between them and me. Yet His voice reached me as if we were standing shoulder to shoulder. "So I have taken matters into My own hands. I will do whatever it takes to fight you. And because you are so small and unprepared, I will win. And then I will fix the Earth My way."

"By reforming the planet and killing everything on it in the process," I said.

"If that is the only way." If He'd had shoulders, He would have shrugged. "Your humans who believe time is linear are charming, but that makes them no less wrong. Creation is a circle, ever renewing itself. Like a dragon eating its own tail. The cycle spirals down to nothingness, and then begins again."

He was coming closer. I had to force myself to stand my ground, so to speak. "We have achieved so much in our time on this planet," I argued. "Yet You would cavalierly toss it all aside – You would deal all of it a death sentence – rather than allowing us puny, pathetic humans the chance to find a solution. You gave us a flawed creation, and now You would take away our chance to fix Your mistake?"

"THE GODS MAKE NO MISTAKES!" He thundered in my ear.

"Don't make me laugh," I said, with way more bravado than I felt. "My parents know Your kind. And if there's one thing they've learned, it's that even a god can be wrong."

"LIES!" He shrieked, and made a beeline for me. He was already close enough that I had to compensate for the column of air He was pushing toward me in order to stay aloft. I realized He intended to knock me out of the sky. So I held my ground until the last possible second. Then, as He opened His maw to rain fire upon me, I darted down and flew below Him – close enough to scorch the tender scales on His belly. He roared and came about, apparently intending to try again to attack me.

And then He stopped dead, and cocked His pointed head. "Listen, little firebird," He crooned. "Can you hear that? Or is your human hearing too pathetically underpowered?"

I ignored the jibe, but stilled my flight. I could indeed hear something, although it was very faint. It sounded like someone calling my name.

It sounded like Mom and Dad calling my name.

What the hell...?

Veles laughed so uproariously that His whole body vibrated, although it still came out sounding like little more than a croak. "Ah, little firebird! I have captured something very dear to you, haven't I?"

"Let them go," I said unsteadily. The sound had been too faint for me to get a fix on them, and now the damned serpent was making too much noise.

"I will not," He said. "Moreover, I will keep taking the things you hold dear until you agree to fight Me. Because while you may have bested Me before now" – I could tell it hurt His pride to admit even that much – "I will win in the end. And then the Earth will be cleansed."

"No," I said, still straining to hear my parents' voices again. "Where are you?" I cried, becoming frantic. "Mom! Dad! Talk to me! I need to know where you are!"

"They are far beyond your reach," He whispered in my ear – and this time He really was next to me. I recoiled, screeching, as once again His eerie, guttural laugh resounded through the air. Then he drew in a huge, sulfurous breath….

And I sat straight up in bed, a cry dying on my lips.

"Sage?" Hilary sounded so sleepy that I doubted she was actually awake.

"Just a nightmare," I told her. "Go back to sleep."

"Mmkay." Her breathing steadied almost immediately.

I threw back my covers and slipped on the sweatshirt I'd worn the day before – although it wasn't the chilly air that was making me tremble. As quickly as I could, I made my way down the hall to the bedroom where my parents had gone to sleep. Calling on all the gods for mercy, I opened the door as softly as I could.

"Who's there?" Mom called out.

I hadn't realized I was holding my breath until I heard her voice. I let it out, and then began to cry. I rushed to the bed and clutched her, and she stroked my hair as she used to do when I was little.

"Naomi?" Dad rolled over. I could see him peering at us by the glow from the bedside clock. "Sage? What is it, sweetheart?"

"I had a bad dream." I wiped my eyes on my sweatshirt sleeve. "It's okay. I'm okay now."

Mom still held on, though. "Let's see if Auntie has any herbal tea." She put a reassuring hand on Dad's arm and walked with me to the kitchen, where she flipped on a light and picked up the kettle that was on the stove.

"I can do that," Auntie said from the doorway as she blinked against the light. "Have a seat, Naomi." Mom did, and Auntie took over both the tea-making and the gentle interrogation. Before I knew it, I had a steaming mug of chamomile tea between my hands, and I'd told Mom and Auntie the whole story.

For some reason, I didn't mind telling Auntie about the dream helmet. Maybe because her son already knew. Not that I was about to tell her how he'd found out.

Mom took a swig of tea and sat back. "Well, clearly, Veles was bluffing about having captured your father and me, because we're still here."

"Yeah."

"Maybe…." Mom traced the flowers on her mug. "Honey, it might have just been a dream. I know how stressful all of this has been for you. And you were pretty upset about Veles knowing about Rafe." She cut a look at Auntie, gauging her reaction to that comment. When Auntie remained calm, Mom went on. "Maybe your subconscious pulled all of this together and put it in a dream. I mean, isn't that what dreams are for? To help us process our feelings about things that have happened to us?"

I shrugged. "Maybe. But it felt pretty real." I remembered the way the dragon's breath smelled, and shuddered. "I don't remember smells registering in any dream I've ever had before."

"Hmm."

"And He gave me a lot of information."

"He didn't tell you anything that we hadn't already figured out, though."

I thought back over the conversation I'd had with the god. "I guess not." I happened to glance at Rafe's mother. She hadn't even touched her tea. "Auntie, you've been quiet," I said. "What do you think?"

Her narrowed gaze took in both of us in turn. "I don't think it was a dream. I think it was real. And He *did* tell us something we didn't know before."

"Oh?" Mom said.

Auntie nodded. "He knows how to get to Sage," she said, pointing her chin toward me. "He knows how to upset her." Her eyes focused on me, and I noticed they were as black and as deep as her son's. "And we know now that He's going to use that knowledge to win."

I sat up and pushed my mug away. "So if Veles actually does capture anyone in my family," I said, "you're saying I shouldn't go after them. Is that right?" I shook my head. "I don't think I can do that."

"Then you'll lose." I heard Mom suck in a breath at Auntie's blunt words, but she went on relentlessly. "Everyone here has more knowledge of the otherworld than you do. Even Webb knows more than you. And every last one of us can get ourselves out of any jam we might find ourselves in on the other side. Your parents have done it countless times."

"I know that," I said, "but...."

"No buts." She slashed downward with the blade of her hand. "If He threatens you with harming anyone you care about, ignore Him. Get in, do your job, and get out. Don't let him get your goat."

I kept my voice as level as my gaze. "What if he takes Rafe?"

She answered me with a hard look. "You let Rafe take care of himself."

We all went back to bed shortly thereafter. You can bet I wore my dream helmet. No amount of embarrassment was worth running into Veles in yet another dream.

The evening before, I had deputized Rafe to find out what was going on with my brother. As we were girding our loins for the big raid that morning, I cornered him. "What's the story?" I asked.

He shrugged. "He won't talk about it. Or at least, he won't talk to *me* about it."

I had just about had enough of subterfuge and denial and all those other things people do to try to spare their loved ones from the worst. "Fine," I said, pushing past him. "He'd damn well better talk to *me*."

I found Webb in the kitchen, pretending to eat a bowl of cereal while he stared out the window at the lightening sky. I made sure to make a lot of noise while I pulled out a chair and sat down in it. "Out with it. What did Kerry say to you?"

He cut a glance at me and resumed chewing. "Nothing."

"You're so full of shit."

"Nothing! It was a private conversation, okay?"

I blew out an exasperated breath. "You're being ridiculous. I *know* what she told you."

"If you know so much," he said, his lip curling, "then why are you bothering me?"

"Because I'd like to help?"

"Nothing will help." He tossed his spoon atop the uneaten cereal. Milk splattered everywhere.

I jumped up to get a sponge. "I've got it."

"No, I've got it." He went so far as to pry the sponge out of my hand. "*I* made the mess. It's my responsibility to clean it up." We glared at one another for a moment, both aware that what he'd just said had nothing to do with spilled milk.

"For gods' sake, Sage," he said with his back to me as he scrubbed the table. "Why do you have to stick your nose in everywhere?"

"Andrew Joseph," I said, aware that I sounded exactly like Mom. "We have kind of a big mission planned for today – one that you insisted you had to be part of."

He glared at me over his shoulder. "I do."

"Well, I can't have a member of the team moping about being rejected when he's supposed to be doing his job!" I'd raised my voice, but at that moment I didn't care who heard us. "Someone could get killed that way!"

"No one's going to get killed," he said, sullen. He sat back down and picked up his spoon again.

"So you say." I resumed my seat. "But you've also said that things can change. Nothing about the future is set in stone."

"None of us will die today," he said again.

That sounded less like a prophecy and more like a statement of fact. "Still…" I went on, pushing him. Then someone put their hands on my shoulders. I sat back in a hurry and craned my neck to see who had the temerity to interrupt my tirade.

"Let it go," Rafe said.

"But…."

"He says he'll be fine." He'd said nothing of the kind, and I opened my mouth to tell Rafe so, but he lay a finger across my lips and turned to my brother. "Don't you?"

"Yeah," Webb allowed. "I'll be fine."

Rafe removed his finger from my mouth. "There," he said. "You see? It's all going to be okay."

Part of me wanted to slap Rafe for interrupting me, and another part of me wanted to kiss him and never let go. I settled for a disgruntled look aimed in Webb's direction. "Just don't do anything to jeopardize the mission," I told him.

He got up and dumped the remainder of his cereal in the sink. Then he turned to us. "Let's just get this over with," he said.

I let out a breath. "I couldn't agree with you more."

Chapter 13

Auntie drove us south of the city along Turnagain Arm toward Girdwood. Rafe and I had passed through the area on our way to Seward, but I had been gawking so hard at the scenery that I hadn't noticed his reaction.

Now, I saw him looking eagerly out the window. He caught me looking at him and shrugged self-consciously. "This is where I grew up," he said.

"Why didn't you tell me that before?" I took a better look out the windows on my side of the car. Ice was collecting along the shore, and the mountains beyond sported mantles of snow. "Is there anywhere in this state that's not beautiful?"

He grinned at me. "Deadhorse is pretty ugly, what with the frozen landscape and all the refineries. Although the weather's better there now than it used to be."

I almost didn't hear him. I was too busy drinking in the sight of snowcapped peaks.

Auntie took a left off the Seward Highway onto a gravel track. As she rounded a bend, I beheld our destination: the unnamed village where she and Rafe had lived when he was small. The ancestral Tlingit homelands were well south of Anchorage, along the south-central coast near British Columbia. But just like everybody else, a lot of Indians had migrated to cities over the years in search of a better life.

The cabins – some little more than shacks – reminded me of the places people used to live in on the Pine Ridge reservation where Grandpa Drew lived. It had gotten a lot better there since the Second Coming. And I could see some improvements happening here, too, particularly in the bold graphics freshly painted on the front of the community house. Three totem poles were attached to the building: one at either of the front corners, and the third and tallest in the middle, with a doorway built into it.

Auntie parked in front of the place and we got out of the car. "This will be our base of operations," she told us. "Joseph and Naomi will wait inside with us. So if you get in trouble, focus on these three totem poles, and they will get you home."

"They're beautiful," Hilary said. "Are those eagles on the top?"

"Bite your tongue," Auntie said with a glint of humor in her eye.

Rafe explained that the Tlingit have two phatries, or sociopolitical divisions. One is the Eagle Clan and the other is the Raven Clan. "We're Raven Clan," he said.

"Naturally," I said under my breath.

He slipped an arm around my shoulders. "So that's Raven at the top of each of those poles."

Hilary nodded. "Nice." *Nahse.*

To keep from whacking myself upside the head, I focused on the base of the central totem pole. "Is that the doorway?" At his nod, I asked, "Why is it shaped like that?"

"Come on," he said. "I'll show you." One by one, we followed him toward the community house.

Each of the totem poles, I noticed as we approached, had been created from the trunk of a single cedar tree. The doorway in the central pole was hand-carved and sanded smooth, and the whole thing was varnished to a sheen. I ducked and stepped up onto the threshold.

A remarkable feeling overcame me as I shuffled through that doorway. It was as if I had passed through a birth canal and was new-made.

Rafe was right behind me. When I mentioned the odd feeling to him, he grinned and said, "I knew you'd get it." He explained that the community gathered here for potlatches and other rituals. The feeling I'd had was intentional; the doorway's design was meant to purify the people attending events in this building as they entered the sacred space inside.

The interior was as memorable as that doorway. The roof was upheld by four pillars, carved in the shapes of what I took to be gods. There was a rectangular fire pit in the very center of the floor, with a skylight that functioned as a smoke hole directly above it. Long benches ran around the perimeter of the pit. At the far end of the building was a raised dais with a screen at the back. The screen was painted with more of the stunning Northwest-Indian-style graphics that depicted various spirit creatures, but I didn't know which was which. "I need to learn more about your mythology," I murmured, and he flashed me a brilliant smile.

The others had joined us at this point. Enkou had apparently met Hilary outside; he trailed behind her now, munching on yet another cucumber, and seemingly unfazed by passing through the community house's symbolic birth canal.

As we all gathered near the pit, Perun materialized on the dais. "Are we all here?" He asked, stepping down to join us.

"We are," said Auntie. I was a little surprised that Mom and Dad were letting her take over. On the other hand, this was her community. On the *other* hand, we're talking about Mom and Dad. Particularly Mom.

"So what's the plan?" I asked. "I mean, I know the broad outlines. We go through the entrance to the underworld, wherever it is" – I cast around for something that would suit for the role, but found nothing other than the front door we'd all been through already – "and find the water Veles is hoarding, and then figure out how to get it back to our world. But we need more detail than that."

"Agreed," said Perun.

"We need a distraction," said Rafe. "Something to lure Veles away from His treasure, so we can find it and set it free." He looked pointedly at me.

"Oh, now, wait a minute," I said.

"A decoy," Perun said, nodding thoughtfully.

"After all," Rafe said, "it's you He wants."

"But...." I stopped myself before I began to babble. Then I forced myself to think about what it was about the suggestion that bothered me so. *He's proposing me as a sacrifice! And I thought he cared about me!*

Well, that was the most visible part of me talking – the shallow part, the part I showed the world. But it didn't feel like the whole reason. So for a moment, I dipped my toes into the darker parts of my psyche – and there it was.

I was mad because *I* was the one who was supposed to save the world. And Rafe's suggestion would put me far, far away from the main action. I'd be distracting the bad guy while someone else saved the day. I'd be on the team, but at the wrong end. Instead of leading, I'd be somewhere else.

Even though I had spent my life rejecting the role I was supposedly born to play, when somebody suggested that someone else play it, it rankled.

Even if it had occurred to me that this gambit might not, in fact, save the world – and might even backfire on us – I don't think I would have been mollified. I was Sage the Savior, damn it. If anybody was going to bring rain back to Earth, it was going to be me.

And besides all of that, to be completely honest, the thought of meeting Veles again terrified me.

Once I figured out the real root of my objection to the plan, my answer was easy. Because I really *didn't* want to save the world. Not if I had to do it by magic. "All right," I said. "What do I do?"

Once I bought into the idea, the rest of the plan fell swiftly into place. Rafe and Perun would come with me to draw Veles away from Nav, while Webb, Hilary, and Enkou descended to Nav to release the water.

I was, as I've said, the bait; Rafe would serve as my reinforcement if things got too hairy, and Perun would step in only if it looked like the dragon was coming close to overpowering us.

"Be careful," Perun told us. "Dragon is only one of His forms."

That was news to me. I'd never seen Him in any other form. "He's a shifter? What other forms can He take?"

Perun shrugged. "Bear. Wolf. Anything. Even human." I couldn't help but glance at my father, who seemed fascinated by the news.

"So basically, then, anybody we meet anywhere could be Veles," Rafe said. "Terrific."

"But He's always appeared to me as a dragon," I argued. "So it would stand to reason...."

"There is no reasoning with Him," Perun broke in. "If He wants something, He will take it. You must fight Him to get it back."

The god sounded almost wistful. I thought about that, and then said, "Look. If You want, I can engage Him first, and then You can step in and land the killing stroke."

He sighed. "Thank you, Sage, but no. For Me, the chase is half the fun."

"Well, okay," I said. "But think about it."

He nodded, and we turned to the role of the rest of the team. We had already figured out that Veles would store the water near the tree's roots, but that root system ranged throughout the world. My parents had run across one of its tendrils in the caves under Grandfather's home, and that hadn't even been part of the main root ball.

Hilary had turned pale. "It sounds like it might take us quite a while to locate the water. How long do y'all think you can keep Veles distracted?"

Rafe and I turned to Perun, who shrugged again. "How long is a thunderstorm?"

"That's not going to be enough time," Webb said. "We're going to need to locate the tank before you guys go up against Veles. We need a scouting expedition. I'll go."

"Webb, you can't," Mom said. I could tell she had been bursting to put in her two cents. "It's too dangerous."

"There's no other way, Mom," he said. "And it's not like I can help the team any other way. Nobody needs a pair of mittens, do they? Or a hat? Maybe an original work of fiber art?" He may have been trying to make a joke, but his tone was bitter.

"Stop it," I said. "We don't have time for you to feel sorry for yourself. Of course, we need you."

"Take Enkou," Hilary said. "He's sneaky. And he's really good at finding water."

All eyes turned to the kappa, who was lying on his back in the fire pit. From his position, it looked as if he'd been trying to look up Auntie's skirt – the idea of which grossed me out. "Yes, please," I said, as Auntie glared at the critter and rearranged her skirt. "Get him out of here."

But Enkou refused to go anywhere without Hilary. With a sigh, she agreed to tag along.

"All right," said Webb, sounding resigned. "Off we go, then, slinking and skulking. Where's this entrance to the underworld?"

"This way," said Auntie, and led us behind the screen at the far end of the hall. There, we saw two doorways. One had a regular standard-size metal door with a doorknob. The other was an elongated oval, similar to the one we had all entered the building through, although smaller. A door made of the same cedar paneling as the rest of the interior fitted the hobbit-hole exactly, so that the doorway was nearly invisible. Between the two doorways was a panel of switches that I assumed controlled the overhead lights.

"Mom, that's a supply cupboard," Rafe said.

"Is it?" She smiled mysteriously and pushed the switch on the far left, and the little door swung open on its own.

Enkou muttered something in Japanese and jumped through the door. "Enkou-san!" cried Hilary, and dove after him.

"Well," Webb said with a crooked smile, "there they go. And I must follow them, for I am their leader." He gave us an ironic wave and crawled through the door.

"I will make sure they stay on track," Perun said, and went after them.

Which left Mom, Dad, Auntie, Rafe, and me staring at one another.

"How long do we wait?" asked Mom. *Before we go in after them*, is what she meant.

"As long as it takes," said Auntie.

"Terrific," I said. "Anybody got a deck of cards?"

It didn't take long. We had moved to the benches around the fire pit, and had barely finished one hand of Spades when our three spies emerged, dripping wet, from behind the screen.

We stood as one. "Looks like you found it," said Rafe.

"Yeah," Webb said, and bent over to catch his breath. He spoke fast, choppy sentences, with a breath in between each one "Hilary's right. Enkou was amazing. He went right to the reservoir. Whew." He straightened and pushed his wet curls up and out of his eyes.

"That's great news," I said, bestowing a smile on Enkou while Hilary gave him a hug.

Auntie produced a cucumber from her tote bag and gave it to the kappa with a bow. He bowed back – although not deeply enough to dump the water from the top of his head – and began gnawing away, apparently oblivious to our conversation.

"So where is it?" Rafe asked. "Is it far?"

"No, not at all," said Hilary. "This portal takes you to a meadow in the Slavic underworld. The world tree's roots look like a network of clouds in the sky. You just trace them to their source – it's not very far. And the reservoir is right close to the trunk of the tree."

"And you're sure it's our water?" I asked. "Not a natural lake or river or something?"

Webb looked at me as if I were a simpleton. "No, Sage," he said patiently. "It's definitely our water."

"It's in a tank with no lid," Hilary added. "The tank looks pretty new, and it goes on forever. We couldn't see the other side of it." She looked to Webb for confirmation, and he gave it with a nod.

I blew out a breath. "So okay. How do we get it back?"

"Enkou dove into the tank to check it out," Webb said. "He says there's a drain plug in the bottom."

"Which leads to…?"

"Our world, with any luck," he said.

"That's not good enough," I said. "What if it doesn't? What if it drains into that meadow you guys had to cross to get there?" I looked at Mom and Dad. "This could be a disaster. We could end up drowning Nav and never get our water back at all."

"Will you relax?" Webb snapped. "Enkou traced the drain pipe. It leads back to the tree and up through the roots. If we pull the plug, we will get our water back."

I traded a look with Rafe. Mine was skeptical. His was not. "That's as good an assurance as we're liable to get," he said. His face was alight with excitement.

I wish I could share it, but something was keeping my enthusiasm banked. Maybe it was the part about me being a sacrificial lamb. Still, we had a job to do, and I'd already agreed to it. "I guess we should go, then. Um." I looked around. "Where's Perun? Did He come back with you guys?"

"We never even saw Him," Hilary said. "Maybe we should wait 'til He comes back."

"He didn't tell us to," Rafe said. "Maybe He's already in Yav, tracking down Veles for us."

"Or maybe he's planning to fight Him Himself," I said darkly. "You saw His expression when He said the chase was half the fun. I don't trust the guy. We need to go." I turned to Webb and Hilary. "You two should wait to pull the plug until we're sure that Veles is distracted. But we need a way to communicate that to you."

"I thought of that." Webb fished in his pocket and pulled out a wad of black yarn. He separated it into two pieces and handed one to Rafe. "Wear this around your neck or something. I'll loop the other one around my wrist. When you're in position, tug on yours. I'll feel it on mine, and we'll send Enkou down to pull the plug."

I glared at my brother while Rafe strung the yarn around his neck. "Why are you giving it to Rafe?" I asked. "Why not me?"

"Because, Sage," he said, as if it were self-evident, "this is yarn. If *you* wear it, it'll burn up."

"Oh," I said, backing down. "I guess that's true."

Rafe finished tying the yarn around his neck and took my hand, apparently unconcerned about our parents' presence. Or maybe he was just too excited to think about it. "Let's go find us a dragon," he said, and led us all behind the screen.

Again, Enkou was first, then Hilary, then Webb. Rafe and I stood outside the doorway for moment. "A kiss for luck?" he said, and fastened his mouth to mine without waiting for a reply.

I pulled away to look at him, trying for some reason to memorize his face: the hooked nose, the dip of hair over his forehead, the sparkling black eyes.

"Ready?" he said.

"No." This time, I kissed him. We were at it for some time.

"For gods' sake, come on!" Webb hissed from the doorway. "I can't believe we're waiting for you while you're standing there, playing tonsil hockey." He rolled his eyes in disgust and crawled back through the hole.

"Coming," Rafe sang out. Then, giggling, we squeezed through the doorway.

Chapter 14

A supply closet, it was not.

The portal led to a tiny chamber with a low ceiling, a dirt floor, and walls of rough-hewn rock. Before us, through another, wider doorway, was a meadow, more beautiful even than the one above Grandfather's old home. Brilliant but diffuse light filtered through the network of roots that formed the canopy of sky high above us. Wildflowers dotted the tall grass, providing spots of startling color amid the green and gold. In front of us, the grasses had been stepped down, making a path. I could see Webb and Hilary some distance ahead. Hilary looked to be chasing something – Enkou, I assumed. Webb turned toward us and waved one arm madly. "Come on!" he yelled, the sound faint, as if coming from very far away.

"I guess we go this way," Rafe said, a wry tone in his voice as he gestured grandly toward the path. I couldn't help grinning as I preceded him through the grass.

"Shouldn't there be people here?" I called over my shoulder as we hiked toward my brother. "I mean, this is the underworld, right? Shouldn't we be meeting spirits or something?"

"It's a big place," Rafe said. "Maybe the spirits all live elsewhere. In Veles's castle or something."

I threw him a startled look over one shoulder. "Veles has a castle?"

"I'd imagine so. He's a god, after all. Don't all gods live in castles?"

This time, I caught the sly tone. "Oh, totally," I said. "Actually, I've never really thought about how the gods live. I guess I've always assumed they sort of dematerialize until the next time humans need them." I glanced back again. "But I guess that can't be true, can it? Some of Them probably believe They deserve to live in splendor, so They do. The Irish gods are said to have homes under the hills there. I'd bet those are pretty posh." I snorted. "And I imagine the Norse deities spend their time in a hall, drinking and swapping war stories."

"What about your parents' gods?" Rafe asked.

"Oh, I imagine White Buffalo Calf Pipe Woman has a tipi of white buckskin to match Her dress."

"And Coyote?"

I flashed him a smirk. "He sleeps anywhere He wants to."

Webb was just ahead of us. His arms were crossed and he wore a thunderous expression. "Took you long enough," he said. He turned on his heel and stalked away from us.

"Hey," I yelled, probably louder than necessary. "Hey, jerkface!" That got his attention. He stopped and pivoted slowly to face me again. "What is your problem?" I said as we caught up to him at last.

"You're taking too long," he said. "Let's go."

Now it was my turn to stop and cross my arms. "No. You're pissed off at me about something, and we need to have it out now. Before your attitude jeopardizes this" – I waved my hands – "project. Mission. Whatever it is."

"I don't want to talk about it."

"Too damn bad." I planted my feet and waited.

He gestured down the path. "Hilary and Enkou are expecting us to be there to back them up!"

"Then you'd better spit it out."

He cast his eyes toward the roof of the underworld and heaved a sigh. When he focused on me again, his eyes were bright with unshed tears. "Why didn't you tell me?"

I had known it was about Kerry, but his accusation stung. "I did tell you," I said. "You chose not to hear me." He opened his mouth to reply, but I stopped him with a gesture. "And I've been telling her for *years* to talk to you. But she kept putting me off. I guess she didn't think I was serious."

"She laughed at me," he said. "She said she could never fall for a guy she considered her little brother." The way he said the words, they sounded like the worst possible insult. Then he mimicked her. "'I love you, Webb, but not *that* way. I couldn't *possibly* love you *that* way.'" I knew he was only exaggerating her tone a little bit. Then he shoved his hands into the pockets of his cargo pants and stared off across the endless meadow.

I reached out to put my hand on his shoulder, but Rafe caught it in his and shook his head wordlessly at me. Then he stepped past me to Webb's side. "That sucks," he said. "I had the same thing happen."

Webb looked at him sidelong. "Yeah?"

"Yeah." The two of them started off down the trail ahead of me. As much as I wanted to eavesdrop to hear Rafe's tale of woe, I forced myself to hang back for a few seconds. I figured the male bonding thing was more important right now. I could get Rafe's story out of him later.

Not long afterward, I began to see a glimmer on the horizon ahead of us. Another few minutes, and I could tell that the glimmer was ambient light reflecting off of a body of water – a *big* body of water. It appeared to stretch from one side of the horizon to the other. A tiny Hilary waved urgently from the edge of the catchment basin. The guys must have seen her, because they stepped up their pace to a jog. I followed suit.

"There you are," Hilary said as we arrived, a little out of breath. "Enkou's disappeared. And I don't want to call his name in case…." She shrieked as the kappa waddled out of the tall grass next to her. "Enkou-san!" she cried, and proceeded to lecture him in Japanese for a good half-minute. He stood impassively while she wound down. Finally she grunted in exasperation and handed him a cucumber.

In the meantime, Rafe put a hand on Webb's shoulder and squeezed. Then he tilted his head toward me.

Webb got the hint. "Sorry, Sage," he said. "I shouldn't have popped off at you like that. It's not your fault Kerry feels the way she does."

I bit back a retort about how Obviousman had just struck again. "It's okay," I said instead. "I should have pushed her harder to talk to you."

"It's okay," he echoed. But he didn't try to hug me. That stung a little bit, but I sucked it up and told myself he would need a little more time to come around.

"So," Rafe said to Webb, "here's the water, obviously. How do we get to Yav?"

In response, Webb pointed a short way ahead. There, what looked like a giant parsnip dangled from the network of roots overhead. The frill of root tendrils at its tip ended scant inches from the edge of the catchment basin.

"That's the taproot?" Rafe asked.

Webb nodded.

"And I'm guessing it would not be good if it reached our water."

"Nope. I mean, I don't know for sure. But it stands to reason."

"So," I said, and stopped. "We have to climb that thing, don't we?"

Rafe gave me a lopsided grin. "I don't see an elevator, so yeah."

But Webb had a better idea. He pulled a new wad of yarn from a pocket and handed it to me. "It's a harness," he said. "It's knotted at one end so you can sit in it, like a chair. Throw the other end over one of the roots near the top and hoist yourself up."

"Brilliant," I said, and meant it. As I stepped into the webbed seat, I said, "Only how are we going to get the other end up there?" But even as I said it, Rafe was shifting. He picked up the loose end in his beak and flew up toward the ceiling.

I glanced back at the root tendrils. I fancied I could see them moving, a fraction of a millimeter at a time, toward our reservoir. I nodded toward the taproot and said to Webb, "I assume you saw where it was the last time you were here. How long do you think we have before this whole operation is pointless?"

"Oh, quite a while," he said. "It probably won't suck the reservoir dry all at once."

"Webb," I said. "How long before it reaches the water?"

He paused. "Maybe an hour or two," he said at last.

"Terrific." I looked up. Rafe had reached the ceiling and was patiently feeding the end of the harness over a branch close to the taproot. When the end dangled from the other side, he grabbed it in his beak again and flew back to us. Then he shifted back and handed the end to Webb, who tied it in a loop around his waist.

"We're going to pull you up," Rafe informed me. "When you get to the top, take off the harness and climb up onto the roots. We'll have to thread our way through to the surface from there."

"Why can't I just fly?" I asked, kicking myself for not thinking of it earlier. "Wouldn't that be quicker?"

"Because if Veles sees your fire, it'll be game over," Webb said. "Just sit back, relax, and enjoy the ride." And the guys began hoisting me into the sky.

I did enjoy the ride. Webb's knotwork held me snugly but not too tightly, and the view was stunning. Looking past the taproot, I could see the whole of the vast catchment basin. Beyond that was a city, and quaint villages of thatch-roofed huts, and something that looked very much like a castle. Apparently Veles lived in style when He wasn't harassing Perun.

Veles probably thought himself quite clever, I realized. He had situated the catchment basin well away from the souls who lived here. What He hadn't known was how close it was to the portal in Rafe's home village.

Unless He did know, and had expected us to use it. But if that were the case, why hadn't He stopped us yet? We'd already used the portal twice. No, He must simply not know of its existence.

That line of speculation was scary enough. But then I noticed the line that was coming down from the roots above, and sucked in a breath. It was fraying badly. It was only yarn, after all, and Rafe certainly hadn't had time to sand the root smooth.

I forgot about the view, and about speculating on whether Veles knew about our portal. In fact, I forgot about everything except watching the yarn that traveled downward as I headed up. In some places, only a single strand of fiber still held.

I reached out and grabbed the line loosely with both hands. If it broke below me, I reasoned, I could grab onto it and pull myself up. Of course, if it broke above me, I was going to be screwed. I wouldn't die – I could always shift and fly the rest of the way – but then Veles would spot us for sure. Game over, as Webb had said.

I looked up. Just a few more yards, and I'd be within the root network. Then I would have more to grab for than a frayed rope. All I had to do was get there.

Three more yards. Two more.

A sturdy root dangled just above my head. If I could bend it down somehow…maybe by breaking it just a little bit….

Fire built behind my eyes. I didn't know whether Veles could sense my laser vision in operation, but I didn't think I had a choice. Narrowing the beam to the width of an X-acto knife, I aimed for the side of the root, as near to the top as I could get from my current angle. I smelled burning wood and cursed under my breath, backing off on the strength of the beam and hoping I wouldn't send the whole tree up in smoke. I didn't know what it would mean for civilization if the World Tree caught fire and burned to the ground, but I was pretty sure it wouldn't be anything good.

I was concentrating so hard on my surgical strike that I almost didn't hear the shout from far below. But my hands felt the line go slack and begin slipping through my hands. I grabbed reflexively and brought myself to a halt, but not before I'd dropped several feet – well out of reach of the root I'd been working on.

I caught my breath and was about to begin hoisting myself up when I felt tension in the line again. Webb and Rafe must have been able to reach the loose end, after all. I wasn't about to trust that yarn, though. I loosened my death grip on the line, gulped, and resumed cutting the root.

The next crack was the root breaking loose. It drooped now, the end just inches above my head. With a small smile of triumph, I let go of the line with my left hand and reached for the branch.

The line chose that moment to snap again. But the branch held.

I wrapped the line around my right fist and began to pull. When I was more or less even with the branch, I swung my legs back and forth in the harness, rocking my feet up toward a likely-looking root.

I nearly lost it when something flickered at the corner of my vision. But it was Rafe in his raven form. He had the loose end of the yarn and got busy tying it securely to another root.

"That...won't help...if it breaks again," I said between swings.

He cawed once, bobbing up and down. Then he flew to the branch I was trying to snag with my feet, and tried to push it closer to me. At last, with a final caw of desperation, he shifted back and grabbed my feet with one hand.

Another few fraught moments, and I was within the relative safety of the root network, perched on a gnarly branch, with Rafe's arms around me. I let out a shaky sigh. "Let's not do that again, okay?"

He laughed. "Okay." He pulled back just far enough so he could see my face. "Gods, Sage. We thought we'd lost you."

"I was never going to fall," I told him. "I would have shifted first. But that was going to be my last-ditch effort. I didn't want to jeopardize the mission."

"Right. The mission." He dropped his forehead against mine for a minute. Then he tugged once on the black choker Webb had given him. He must have received a tug in return, because he sat back. "Ready?"

"Sure." I chanced a look down, but the root network obscured my view of the taproot's bottom. "How much time do we have, anyway?"

He shook his head. "Not much."

"Terrific." I scrambled to my feet, ducking under the trailing roots, and slid out of what was left of the harness. I considered tossing it down to the ground, but I wasn't sure whether I had a clear shot – and we might need it again on the way back. Although how it would do us any good with the line so frayed, I wasn't sure. Maybe

Webb could repair it while he and Hilary waited for us to engage Veles.

"How are your jungle gym skills?" Rafe asked.

I looked up into what seemed like an endless network of roots. "I guess we're going to find out." And I began to climb, with Rafe right behind me.

It seemed to take forever, but at last daylight began to break through. "Nearly there," Rafe said, when I nearly lost my footing on a root for the fifth or sixth time.

"Good," I replied, out of breath. I had been running on adrenaline for too long. First the harrowing ascent from Nav, and now this interminable climb.

But Rafe was right. Just another few feet, and we emerged from the base of the tree together. "Shit," I said as I looked around. I swayed against him and held on. We weren't in the gods' domain any more; we were in Yav. In our reality. And I had been in this place before.

"I knew it," said Rafe. He pointed at the mountains looming to our right. "That's the Brooks Range. And over there is Barrow." He gestured vaguely to the left; I could see smudges of industrial smoke on the horizon. "Which means...." He turned to look behind us and stopped. "Hello, Dad."

I wheeled around. Striding toward us was a tall, thin man in a black jacket made from some state-of-the-art fabric. Salt-and-pepper hair peeked out from under a Russian-style fur hat. As he got closer, I began to see the family resemblance: Rafe had inherited his hooked nose and black eyes. But the older man's face was longer and thinner, and the corners of his mouth turned down in what seemed to be a habitual expression of distaste. "Rafe." He nodded to his son, and then to me. "You must be Sage. I'm Ben Orloff." Then he half-turned. "And I believe you have already met my associate."

I followed his gaze, and my knees turned to jelly. For bringing up the rear was the giant serpent I'd begun to hate.

"So, little firebird," He purred. "We meet again."

My mind reeled. Veles was Rafe's father's god? Why hadn't he told me?

Maybe he didn't know. But maybe he did. After all, he'd known that Perun was his brother's god, but hadn't shared it with me.

Did Auntie know? She must know about Ben Orloff's connection to Veles – she herself had a connection to deity, and I knew she wasn't stupid.

But…Perun and Veles? Rafe's brother and his father? Was this just some kind of family feud with global implications?

What made them decide to suck me into this?

Why hadn't Rafe *told* me?

I backed away. I couldn't trust any of them. And everyone I could trust – Mom, Dad, and Grandfather – was thousands of miles away.

Even Webb was somewhere far below us. And Rafe had our only means of communicating with him.

"Sage," Rafe said, taking a step toward me. "It's not what you think."

"I don't know what to think," I said.

"Sage, no," he said again, taking another step.

"Don't come any closer," I said, throwing my hands up in front of me.

"Don't do this," he said.

"Don't do what?" I said. "Look, you're the one who got me involved in all of this. You're the one who dragged me up here without telling me what was going on. Did you *know* your father was allied with Veles? Did you know the World Tree would lead us here?" The tree! I looked around. There was no towering oak anywhere nearby. No massive root system to climb back down into. Nothing but tundra and caribou, a settlement that was much too far away, and the mountains.

Mountains, I understood.

"Listen to me!" Rafe pleaded.

I went on as if I hadn't heard him – or as if I'd heard, but it didn't matter. "There's no way out, is there?" I said. "You and your family have engineered this whole thing perfectly. You've isolated me here, at the end of the Earth, and set me up so that I'll have to fight my way out." I chuckled mirthlessly. "What an idiot I was. I thought you cared for me."

"I do," he said, a catch in his voice. Oh, he was good. "I do care for you. Don't do this," he said again.

"I have to," I said. "I don't have any choice. The only way home is through the fire." As I spoke, I shifted, and launched myself into the sky. I wheeled over them, shedding sparks, and raced away.

"Don't leave me!" Rafe pleaded as I zoomed away. "Don't leave me here with them!"

I could barely hear him over Veles's booming laughter.

But I couldn't go back. I had already set my course for the safety of the mountains. And while part of me gibbered about how I was abandoning Rafe, I forced myself to take comfort in Auntie's advice: *Let Rafe take care of himself.*

Chapter 15

I flew as if the hounds of Hell were on my tail. But while Veles's laughter followed me, the god Himself did not. I was too rattled to wonder what that meant.

Upon reaching the foothills, I began to look for a place to hide. The first thing I spotted looked too much like the lair that Veles had slithered out of when I'd first met Him in my dream. It might have been a coincidence, but I wasn't going to take the chance.

I flew farther south, catching air currents when I could find them. My resources were just about at their limit. I could feel my wings tremble with exhaustion on every downbeat.

At last, I spotted a crevice that I thought would do the trick. I landed, stumbling wearily to the wall, and poked my head through the crack. I was finally in luck. My fiery headgear illuminated a cave, perhaps six feet deep and apparently unoccupied. Sagging gratefully against the rock face, I shifted back to my human form and dragged myself through.

The cave was cool and dim. I collapsed against the far wall and lay prone on the rock for a few moments. But only a few – I was sure Veles had marked my burning trail across the sky, and was even now plotting ways to draw me out for whatever evil purposes He and Rafe's father had in mind.

I didn't know why, but for some reason, Grandfather's comment about Veles occurred to me. *He is not evil*, the old man had said, and he would have had no reason to lie. In fact, I knew that none of the gods were evil. My parents had taught me that evil was a human concept – that the gods generally just did what They thought was best, for reasons which They considered to be justifiable at the time. The gods certainly could be mischievous, and were capable of being capricious. But evil? Almost never.

Yet every time I had run into Veles, He had struck me as having a streak of evil.

I was far too tired to ponder this paradox. I had meant to rest for just a few moments, and then figure out what to do next. Tops on my list was survival. Keeping warm wouldn't be an issue – even if I found no firewood, I could heat up rocks. But I would need food pretty soon. And water. I was already thirsty. And we had left the community house with no supplies.

"Need to get up and find water," I mumbled as my eyes drifted shut.

I became aware of a glow emanating from the back of the cave. Curious, I got to my feet and moved cautiously toward the light.

It was coming from a narrow back exit. I squeezed through the slit and found myself in a spacious passageway with a gentle downward slope. Some distance ahead, the passage took a right turn. The light was coming from that direction. Again, I followed it.

Around the bend, I found myself in a grotto. A deep pool of precious water stretched before me, tinged green and lit from below with a buttery yellow light. I felt a splash on my forehead, and looked up to see water dripping from stalactites high above. I knelt at the edge of the pool with a grateful sigh and scooped up water with my hands until my thirst was satisfied.

When I sat back, I realized I wasn't alone.

"My child," said the goddess seated next to me. I knew Her at once. She was heavily pregnant with the Earth – it shone like a blue-and-white marble through the greenish skin of Her naked belly.

"Gaia," I said, and scrambled to my feet. "I'm sorry. I didn't realize…."

"Please, Sage," She said with a smile, Her hand gesturing gracefully to the place I'd just vacated. "There is no need for you to go. You are always welcome here."

Wobbling a little, I sat back down. Then I began to cry.

"Oh, My child," said Gaia, and enfolded me in Her arms. "Tell Me what is troubling you."

So I did. I told Her the whole thing – how Veles had stolen the rain and snowmelt, how Rafe had tricked me, and how I was trapped here without anyone I could trust. "Except You, of course," I said hastily, as I wiped my nose on my sleeve. "I'm sorry. I wanted to save the Earth my way, and instead I've made a mess that I don't know how to fix. And now I've invaded Your sacred space and dumped the whole thing in Your lap."

Gaia was frowning. "This does not sound like the Veles I know. His rule of Nav is both generous and just. He presides over music and is kind to sheep. I have never known Him to be cruel. And He is certainly not evil."

"Grandfather said the same thing," I said. "That Veles isn't evil, I mean. He's the yang to Perun's yin, but good and evil don't enter into it."

"Looks Far is a wise man." Gaia looked away, into the shadows on the other side of Her pool. "But then the question is: if the entity working with Rafe's father is not Veles, who is it?"

My eyes widened. I'd been so upset about Rafe lying to me that I hadn't considered the possibility of Veles being an impostor. Maybe Rafe hadn't lied to me. He wasn't exactly close to either his father or his brother. Maybe he really hadn't known any more than I did.

And then I remembered how I'd last seen him – pleading with me not to abandon him – and I went cold all over. "Whoever this fake Veles is, He's got Rafe," I said.

She looked at me sharply. "Well, we need to get him back, don't we?" She tapped one slim finger against Her chin. "First things first. I will alert your parents as to what has happened, and put the word out amongst the gods. Especially Perun."

"He was supposed to meet us here," I said. "But He never showed."

"And that is very unlike Him. I fear He, too, has been hoodwinked by the impostor. I would wager He is waiting for you in the place where He usually battles Veles, and is wondering why you have not yet come." She stood. "Where do you suppose this impostor would have taken your friend?"

"Probably the cave where I first saw Him in my dream," I said, and described it to Her as well as I could.

"I can find it," She said, and stooped to place a kiss on my forehead. "Sleep now, My child. You will need your strength for what lies ahead."

"All right," I said. I meant to thank Her, and then get up and make my way back to my own little cave. But my eyelids were so heavy that I stretched out on the pool's edge.

I awoke with a start, and groaned. Every muscle in my body hurt – not surprising, given the workout I'd had the day before. And solid rock is not the most forgiving of mattresses. I pushed myself up to a seated position and stretched some of the kinks out.

I froze when my leg connected with something soft. I turned my eyes on low – just enough to dispel the worst of the shadows – and discovered someone, or more likely Someone, had deposited a water skin next to me on the cave floor. Gratefully, I unstopped the skin and drank a few sips – just enough to get the taste of sleep out of my mouth. Then I slipped the water skin's strap over my head and squeezed out of the cave.

It was night – clear and cold. I crossed my arms and scanned the skies in wonder. Even at home, I never saw this many stars. Their light revealed nothing but peaks and steep cliffs around me.

I'd flown pretty far into the mountains to escape Veles, and had not been in the best of shape to be navigating at the time. So I had only a vague idea of where I was. And I had no idea about what was happening elsewhere. Had Gaia gotten hold of my parents? Had Rafe signaled to Webb to let the water go? Were Webb and Hilary okay?

Was Rafe okay?

I didn't know what anyone else was up to, but I knew what I had to do next. Hoping that the water skin was fireproof, I shifted and took to the sky.

I knew I would be visible for miles around – a streak of orange fire against the black night sky – but at that moment, I didn't care. I'd abandoned Rafe, who cared for me. Auntie's advice be damned – I needed to do whatever was necessary to get him back.

It took me only a few minutes to reach the northern side of the Brooks Range. Barrow was a faint glow on the northern horizon to my right as I scanned the hills to my left for the configuration of boulders I remembered. But either the light was insufficient or the angle was too different, or both.

With my anxiety increasing, I somersaulted to make a pass in the opposite direction – and noticed something moving on the tundra. Several somethings, in fact. Caribou? After dark? No, their movement was wrong – instead of galloping or loping, these creatures appeared to be undulating.

Kind of like Veles in his dragon form.

And now I saw a hovercar – a more utilitarian model than the one my parents owned – speeding after them. I landed on the nearest promontory and shifted to douse my light and watch. I didn't think they had noticed me yet, and I didn't want to take any chances. The cold night air hit me at once, making me shiver. I crouched to conserve body heat and rubbed my hands on my upper arms while I watched the show.

In moments, a second hovercar joined the first. The two vehicles split up and flew around the fleeing specimens on either side. I'd seen cowboys herding cattle in southern Colorado, and I was pretty sure that's what the guys piloting the hovercars were up to.

I looked back the way the cars had come. Not far away was a miniature village of old-time Quonset huts, complete with lights above every door.

And here came the giant worms again, heading back toward the Quonset huts, with the hovercars in pursuit.

I glanced over my shoulder at the Brooks Range, and back at the makeshift village. Then I stood up and began picking my way down the slope. If Veles was holed up in the mountains, Gaia would find Him. But I was looking for whoever was holding Rafe – and my money was on the worm cowboys.

At least the walk warmed me up a little. But my teeth were still chattering when I reached the edge of the camp. If I'd had more time, I could have staked out the place, watched comings and goings, and figured out which building he was being held in.

Of course, if I'd had a giant can opener, I could have just popped the top off of each building in turn until I found him. But I lacked both time and useful tools, so I was going to have to make an educated guess.

Just as I thought of that giant can opener, my father's words echoed in my head: *Always look for the quickest way out.* I grinned to myself. I might not have a giant can opener with me, but I came self-equipped with the next best thing.

The cowboys had long since parked their hovercars, corralled their charges in one of the largest huts, and headed off to two of the smaller huts nearby. I presumed those two were barracks or dorms. A fourth building appeared to be the mess hall, judging by the overflowing trash containers outside. That left six huts to check out – and in front of one of them was a fellow in a parka, pretty obviously standing guard.

Ding ding ding.

I scooted around to the back of the hut. Then I set my eyes on low beam and went to work on the back wall. As I made the cuts, the corrugated metal began rolling back onto itself. Mindful of the glowing-hot edges, I slipped inside.

Rafe, bound and gagged, was in the corner. His temple glistened in the dim light, and as I got closer, I realized it was bloody. His eyes were wide open in fear.

My heart clenched as I reached behind his head to loosen the gag. "I'm so sorry," I whispered, fumbling with the knot. My fingers were nearly numb with cold.

He shook the gag loose. "What are you doing here?" he said. "Get out! Run!"

I sat back in surprise. "I'm not leaving without you." Then I began working on the rope binding his hands.

"No," he moaned softly. "You don't understand."

"You're right. I don't. And you're going to explain it to me as soon as we're away from here."

"Sage," he whispered urgently. "Veles isn't who we thought he was."

"Yeah, I know," I hissed back. "Gaia figured it out."

"Gaia?" he murmured, surprised.

I put a finger to my lips. "I've had a busy night. Help me with this." I'd loosened the rope on his wrists and began working on the one around his ankles. Then I paused to look more closely at the wound on his temple. "Are you okay?"

He didn't answer my question. Instead, he hissed, "Sage, you need to leave!"

"Not without you," I said, as the rope around his ankles came free. "Let's go." I grabbed his hand to help him up. When he didn't move, I glared at him. "Don't you want to leave?"

"Of course I want to leave!" He seemed to be on the verge of tears.

"Well, come on!" I tugged again on his hand. This time, he got to his feet and followed me through the tiny doorway. Hand in hand, we fled across the tundra to the relative safety of the hills.

We paused at last behind a pile of rocks, our labored breaths steaming. I noticed the outlines of things were clearer. "Dawn's coming."

"Yeah." The wound on his temple still bled. I fished a tissue from my jeans and reached up to blot at it, but he batted my hand away fiercely. "Don't touch it!"

I recoiled. Then my eyes narrowed. "Why?" When he remained silent, I said, "Tell me what they did to you!"

His shoulders sagged. "They infected me."

"Infected...?"

He nodded. "With a kind of worm that lives in the ice up here. It lives on a certain kind of bacteria, and it's...mutated...to reproduce in human flesh." He avoided looking at me. "The larvae cause changes in the human cells they inhabit. Eventually, the host mutates into…."

"A giant flying worm," I said. "Jesus, Rafe. We've got to get that thing out of you."

He shook his head. "There's only one person in the world who knows how."

"Who?"

"My father."

My eyes went wide. "Well, come on, then! He's up here, right? Let's find him and get it done!"

But Rafe had not stopped shaking his head. "He won't do it, Sage. He's not going to help me."

His own *son*? "Why the hell not?"

At last, he looked at me. "Because he's the one who put it in there."

I didn't know what to say. His own *father…*?

We might have gone on standing there, staring at each other, until the end of time, or at least until Rafe mutated into a giant worm before my eyes. But Gaia materialized next to us, took our hands, and brought us back to the community house.

Auntie took one look at Rafe's temple and began screaming.

Before you ask...

I have no excuse for not knowing that the giant slug Sage had ID'd as Veles was an impostor. Maybe if I'd been paying more attention, I would have known. But thanks to Kerry, I was too preoccupied with my own misery. And that only got worse after the yarn harness failed. If I'd been thinking straight, I would have realized the material for the harness was all wrong – too stretchy and too easily frayed. If I'd thought ahead, I would have stashed some climbing rope in one of the pockets of my cargo pants. But I spent the last few minutes at home with Kerry, and after that conversation, all thought of proper preparation went out of my head.

And it nearly got Sage killed. Oh, I know she could have shifted and flown to safety. But I've seen her under pressure: sometimes she has the presence of mind to do that sort of thing, and sometimes she doesn't. Either way, it was my job to keep her out of danger – or at least, to minimize the danger she was in. And I didn't do it.

So yeah, between the depression over what Kerry had said and the self-flagellation over what I'd almost done to Sage, I wasn't really at my best.

And then there was Enkou. Hilary and I tried to keep an eye on him, but he kept wandering away from us. When I thought about it later, I realized he was just doing his job, or what he perceived to be his job. He was investigating the catchment basin, learning all he could about the structure. But after all the shenanigans he'd pulled on campus, Hilary didn't trust him. She kept trying to get him to stay with us, at least until we got a message from Rafe.

I have to give Hilary credit for one thing – she and Enkou were the only things keeping me in the game. We had way too much downtime, sitting next to that catchment basin. If I had been by myself, I might have worked myself into a funk so deep that jumping into the catchment pond taking a deep breath would have sounded like a good idea. But I couldn't be that morose – not with Hilary jumping up every few minutes to scan the nearby field for the kappa. She would stand on her tiptoes and yell, "Enkou-san!" at the top of her lungs, and eventually he'd show up and they'd bitch each other out in Japanese. Then he would sit next to us in the grass, shooting her disgruntled looks, until her attention wavered. Then he'd take off again. A few minutes later, she'd realize he was gone, and the whole cycle would start over.

I admit that a couple of times, I saw him take off. I could have told her right away, but I thought it was more fun to let her figure it out on her own. And anyway, I didn't want to alienate Enkou by ratting him out. Plus it gave Hilary and me some time to talk.

It turned out that she had more of an artistic soul than my sister did, which admittedly isn't saying much. But it still surprised me that a math major – okay, statistics, same difference – would be interested in anything creative.

"But you use math in your work," she insisted at one point.

"I most certainly do not." I shuddered for effect.

"Yes, you do," she said. "You have to figure out length and width for your projects, right? And tolerances, to make sure things will fit?"

"Yeah," I said. "So?"

"So that's math," she said triumphantly. "Actually, come to think of it, it's physics."

"You mean I'm doing science, too?" I said, letting my voice squeak a little bit. "This is all very disheartening."

She had cocked her head and was squinting at me a little. "You know what I think?" she said. "I think you're smarter than you let on, Webb Curtis."

No, that would be Kerry. Which reminded me that I was supposed to be depressed. So I changed the subject.

It was hard to gauge the passage of time in Nav. It's not like we could see the sun making its way across the sky or anything. But eventually I realized hours must have passed since Rafe and Sage had disappeared among the roots of the World Tree.

When I mentioned it to Hilary, she told me she had been wondering the same thing. "Maybe you should tug on your necklace," she suggested.

"Good idea," I said, and tugged. No response. I tried it again, and then a third time. Each time, I yanked a little harder. And each time I received no answering tug, her eyes got a little rounder.

At last, she said, "Something's happened. Let's go back to the community house and see whether your folks have heard anything."

"Sounds like a plan," I said. She stood to round up Enkou, and I wondered what awful thing was happening that I hadn't been able to foresee.

Chapter 16

Rafe said the project had started out innocently enough. His father was a biologist who specialized in the study of life forms whose existence depended on fossil fuels like petroleum and methane. "Like methane ice worms," Rafe said. We were sitting on the benches around the community house fire pit, surrounded by the remains of the picnic lunch Auntie had packed the day before. "They live on deposits of methane molecules that have been trapped in ice on the ocean floor. We've discovered that they feed on a specific kind of bacteria that lives only in the presence of both methane and ice."

"Charming," I said. I couldn't let go of his hand.

"Yeah. Anyway, my father was fascinated by these kinds of symbiotic relationships, and began studying them for potential application in the oil and gas industry. And then he ran across this particular worm. It lives only in the shelf ice at the edge of the Arctic Ocean, and only in proximity to deposits of natural gas. Dad thought he might be able to genetically engineer the worm to drill into the ice and release the gas. Then all we'd have to do is run a pipeline to collect the stuff the worms released."

"Did it work?" Webb asked. He and Hilary, concerned that they hadn't heard from us, had returned through the portal several hours after we'd disappeared into the World Tree's roots. Then Perun came in and said we had never showed up at the rendezvous point. Mom, Dad, and Auntie had been pretty frantic until Gaia arrived.

"Depends on your definition of success," Rafe said. "Dad was working with another scientist – a guy named Vasily Dubchov. Vasily had an open sore on his hand – he'd scraped it while retrieving the test subjects from the ice. He must have picked up some worm food when he hurt himself, because the worms went for his wound. Absolutely swarmed him. And one of them burrowed right into it." Rafe said all of this calmly, which only added to the ick factor.

"And Ben just let it happen," Auntie said, as if she had expected no less. "I remember this. You told me about it when you came back home that summer." She had hold of Rafe's other hand.

"He didn't just let it happen," Rafe said. "He talked Vasily into being a test subject. To see what would happen if they left the worm in there."

"And what happens," said Webb, "is that people turn into giant ice worms."

"Right. But they keep their higher thinking processes, as well as their ability to burrow through ice. They basically morph into the perfect miners for fossil fuels trapped in ice."

"But they're slaves," Hilary said, horrified. "Mutated slaves."

"We have to stop this," Mom said. "Why hasn't anyone shut this project down yet?"

"They've been keeping it quiet," said Rafe. "Vasily was attacked about five years ago."

"Right," said Auntie. "When Rafe told me about it, I had a little discussion with Ben." Her expression indicated it was more than a little discussion. "I asked him a number of questions that he didn't have good answers for. After that, I said Rafe couldn't spend any more summers with him."

"And Dad told me he was okay with that – that he was too busy with the game-changing project he was involved in. I didn't learn any of the details until last night." He looked at me. "The guy who claimed to be Veles? That's Vasily. There's a psi ability that comes along with the physical mutation. That's how he was able to get into your dreams."

I shuddered. "Why's he after me?"

"Because the transformed humans can't stand the cold as well as the worms can. And you're supposed to save the Earth from climate change. If the Arctic gets too cold, the project will be dead."

"Good," Auntie said. She punctuated her comment by giving Rafe's hand a decisive shake.

"It's always about money, isn't it?" Mom said with a sigh.

Rafe said carefully, "I think, for my father, it started out being about the science. It was Vasily who was more interested in a big payout. And now, Dad doesn't want to see his life's work destroyed."

"I don't think there's any way to keep that from happening," I said.

"We need to get the gods involved in this," Mom said. "And we need to get that thing out of your head, Rafe. How long before it starts mutating?"

He winced, but replied, "I don't know."

"Any idea what the first signs are?" That was my father.

"No."

"We need more information," Mom said, "and we need to convince Rafe's father to remove that thing. Why did he infect you with it, anyway?"

Rafe looked at me. "To lure Sage back to the camp, of course. And it worked."

"But they didn't count on me busting you out," I said. That got me a small smile.

"Wait," said Webb. "If Vasily's not a god, then how did he set up the catchment basin in Nav?"

"That was My fault," said a new voice, as two gods strode out from behind the panel behind the dais. One was Perun, and He had a tight hold on the other god's arm. The newcomer had wooly hair and a long, tangled beard. Curly ram's horns adorned His head, and a bearskin cloak stretched across His shoulders. This, at last, was Veles.

Perun nudged Him. "Tell them what You did. Go on."

Veles glared back at Him. "Yes, all right. Let go of Me, will You?"

"No tricks, Veles."

"All right! All right!" He replied in exasperation.

Perun grunted and relented His hold on the underworld god, who twitched His cloak back into place before turning to us. "Vasily came to Me last winter, and talked Me into...."

"Veles," Perun said in warning.

"Oh, very well," said Veles. "The truth, then. Vasily is a *vodyanoi*." Seeing our blank faces, He explained impatiently, "A water sprite. Honestly, Perun, how do You expect Me to...."

Perun fingered the haft of the axe at His belt.

Veles rolled His eyes and got on with it. "Fine. Vasily came to Me last winter with plans for a large water tank for his cattle. He wanted to build the tank in Nav so the other *vodyanye* couldn't get to it and steal his water. He told Me he would be siphoning water from Yav to fill the tank, but he didn't tell Me where he was going to take it from. And frankly, I didn't care. The thought of outwitting those stupid, drunken *vodyanye* appealed to Me, so I told him to go ahead. And then, to be honest, I forgot all about it." He glared at Perun. "Until Mr. Muscle here showed up on My doorstep."

"But now that You know the truth," Perun said, "You'll help set things right. Won't You?"

"Yes, of course," Veles said, rolling His eyes. "I will release the water. And I will deal with Vasily."

"Vasily first," Mom said. "Rafe needs help, and fast."

Veles squinted at Rafe for a moment. Then His eyes went wide. "Oh, My dear boy. Who has done this to you?"

"My father," said Rafe bitterly. "Who's with Vasily."

Veles nodded sympathetically. "Then yes, that must be the first order of business." He looked at my father. "Coyote, I have a plan."

"I was hoping You'd say that," Dad said. Beside him, Mom rolled her eyes. I couldn't help but grin at the two of them, and I looked at Webb to share the family moment. But he was digging in his pockets again.

"Here," he said, extending a wad of yarn to Dad. "Take this. It's a net. It might come in handy."

"Thanks, son." Dad gave him a smile as he stuffed it into his jeans pocket. "Why don't you and Hilary go back down to the catchment basin and...." He looked around. "Where's Enkou?"

Hilary's shoulders sagged, her face a mask of annoyance. Then she went for the portal. Webb shook his head and followed her.

"They'll be fine," Mom said to Dad, although she didn't sound convinced. "Just go and help Rafe."

"Are you coming?" Dad asked her. "We could use your negotiating skills."

"All right," she said as she stood, suppressed excitement in her voice. She gestured toward Auntie and continued, "Sadie should come, too. Maybe she can talk some sense into Ben." Then she turned to me. "Sage, you stay here."

"Oh, no, you don't," I said, surging to my feet. Gods and humans alike turned to me in surprise. "You're doing it again!" I said to my parents. "You can't just take over! This is *my* mission, remember?"

They traded a look. "But honey, we just want to keep you safe," Mom said.

"You can't," I said. "You can't lock me away in a tower and believe the gods will never find me there. You, of all people, know that's not the way it works. And anyway, Rafe is my...." I stuttered to a halt. What was he to me, anyway? Friend? Friend with benefits? Love of my life? This seemed like a bad time to go fishing for a label to put on our relationship.

He didn't seem to need one. Wordlessly, he raised our still-joined hands and kissed the back of mine. Then he turned to my parents and said, "She's coming. Or I'm not."

"Kids today," Dad said, the corners of his mouth quirking up. "You should have raised her better."

"Oh, like you had nothing to do with it," Mom retorted. "Let's go."

And just like that, the seven of us were on the tundra near Barrow.

"Shit," I said quietly to Rafe. "We forgot to bring coats again."

He shivered. "Let's hope this doesn't take long."

I couldn't help glancing at the wound on his temple. "Yeah. How do you feel?"

"Okay so far." But his tone was hesitant. I would have probed more thoroughly, but Dad approached us at that moment to outline the plan he and Veles had cooked up. It sounded crazy to me, but I had a history of believing anything to do with the gods was crazy. Dad seemed to think it would work – and I wanted to believe him. In fact, I wanted nothing more than to wrap this up and go back to school. Back to my house in Boulder. Back to having coffee with Rafe after Water Chem. Back to normal.

I should have known better. As soon as the gods get involved, "normal" is a thing of the past.

Mom, Auntie, Rafe, and I took our places next to the Quonset hut that housed Ben Orloff's lab. It gave us a great view of the vacant land in front of the camp – the site Dad and the gods had chosen for the big confrontation.

In the middle of that patch of tundra, Veles materialized. He was in his dragon form – and now I saw my mistake. Veles's dragon was easily twice as large as Vasily's. He retained the wooly hair and beard, and the ram's horns. But instead of Vasily's clumps of cilia, Veles had a long, dorsal fin that helped Him slice through the air. And also unlike Vasily, Veles had hands.

"Vasily!" He roared. "You lazy sot! You pathetic excuse for a *vodyanoi*! I will speak with you!"

I heard noise from the large hut to my right – the one the cowboys had herded the giant worms into. One of the roll-up doors was opening, and Vasily slithered out. "My lord Veles?" he called, sounding cordial. "This is an unexpected pleasure. What brings You to Yav?"

"You and your sick plans, that's what," Veles snapped. "I have only just now learned of how you tricked Me in order to lure that young woman here. You are perverting Yav with your schemes, Vasily. And all for what? Profit?" He boomed a laugh. "You think profit in this world will buy you a fine house in Nav?"

"I do not mean to die," Vasily said equably. Behind him, I saw my father – Webb's net in one hand – slip into the hut through the door the giant worm had left open.

"Even *vodyanye* die," said Veles, advancing toward Vasily.

"That isn't what I meant," said Vasily. The commotion was drawing spectators. Perhaps eight or ten men straggled out of the huts I'd taken for barracks and were gathering along the fence that surrounded the paddock where Vasily held court.

"But it is what *I* meant," Veles said calmly. At that moment, Perun appeared in midair above Vasily. He brought down His axe on Vasily's head, splitting his skull in two and laying him out flat. The blow rocked the tundra like an earthquake, and the resulting peal of thunder would have been enough to wake the dead.

That brought Ben Orloff out of his hut at last. He yanked the door open and took several steps toward the paddock, bellowing, "Vasily! What the devil's going on out there?"

I stepped up next to him. "The devil has nothing to do with this, Mr. Orloff," I said.

A grin overspread his face. "Ah, the little firebird has returned, after all. What a mistake." He grabbed my upper arm roughly and was about to pull me back into his lab, but Rafe blocked his way.

"No, Dad," he said. "The mistake is yours."

His father sneered at him. "Get out of my way, Rafe. You can't stop me."

"He's not alone," said Auntie, as she and Mom took up the last of the compass points surrounding him. "What have you done to our boy, Ben? You promised me you wouldn't hurt him!"

"He's not a boy any longer," he said, his voice rough. "He's a man. And a brilliant scientist. You should never have sent him away. He needs to be here, with me, helping me with my work."

"Your work destroys the planet," Rafe said, a hard edge to his black eyes. "I want to save it. I told you that."

"And so you hitched your star to hers." He squeezed my arm harder. "A brilliant move, Rafe. Just stunning. The only trouble is that she isn't going to save anything. She's only going to make things worse." He pulled me around so that I was in front of him. "Look at her! *She's* supposed to save the planet? She's just a girl relying on fairy dust!"

"You're wrong," Rafe said, anger suffusing his face. "You don't know anything about Sage. She's an environmental engineer, and a brilliant scientist in her own right. She's not going to use any mumbo-jumbo to save us." Then he winced, and I realized it wasn't emotion that was making his face turn red.

"No!" I cried. Fire built behind my eyes, and I channeled it into my skin. Rafe's father yelped in pain and released me. I wheeled on him. "Get that thing out of him!"

He put his injured hands into his armpits and cringed away from me. "I can't," he said. "It's too late. The larvae are invading his cells."

Rafe cried out, the wound at his temple oozing fresh blood. Auntie whimpered and gathered him into her arms. She looked at Rafe's father, accusation in her eyes. "How could you do this to your own son?"

Guilt flickered on his face. It was there and gone in an instant, but it was all the opening Mom needed. "Mr. Orloff," she said, "do you have an antidote?"

He looked at her sidelong. "Yes, but…."

She gave him the full-bore stare. "Use it."

Even I could feel that *push*. Rafe's father had no chance. He turned on his heel and headed back into the lab. "Bring the boy," he said over his shoulder.

With Auntie supporting Rafe, the four of us followed him in, and shut the door behind us.

"Get him up on the table," Rafe's father said. He went to a cabinet on the wall and put his eye up to the retinal scanner next to the handle. The device beeped twice and the door swung open.

In the meantime, Auntie had backed Rafe up to the exam table. His skin had taken on a dusky red hue, and he had raised his arms to cover his head. I ran to help, and together we managed to get him onto the table. He promptly pulled himself into a fetal position, his arms still holding his head. He hadn't made a peep since his cry outside. That scared me most of all.

"Pull his arms down," Mr. Orloff said brusquely, a hypodermic in one hand. Auntie and I each took a hand, but Rafe wouldn't let us move them. "I need to get to the entry wound," he said. "Pull his arms down!"

Auntie and I shared a despairing look, but we redoubled our efforts, and managed to pry his arms far enough apart to reveal the pulsing wound. A sickly purple fluid was beginning to drain from it, trickling toward his ear.

Mr. Orloff jammed the hypo into the wound. Rafe screamed and went rigid. Then all of his muscles went slack.

"What have you done?" Auntie cried.

Mr. Orloff pulled out the needle and ejected it into a biohazard container. "I gave him the antidote," he said. He placed two fingers to his son's throat, feeling for a pulse. Then he sagged back, muttering, "I hope it was in time."

Dark purple slime gushed from the wound. Auntie grabbed a white cloth from a bin next to the table and began to blot it up.

The door slammed open and Dad rushed in. "What the hell?" he yelled.

"It's all right, Joseph," Mom said. "Rafe's been given the antidote. Close the door."

He did, and then he gave Mom a hug. Then he crossed to me and put his arms around me. That's when I realized I was shaking. I buried my face in my father's shoulder and hung on.

"He'll sleep now," Mr. Orloff said as he washed his hands.

"What's going on out there?" Mom asked.

Over my head, Dad said, "Webb's net worked perfectly. I was able to capture all of the worms in it. And Perun's got the human crew corralled."

"What about Vasily?" Mr. Orloff said. He had shut off the water, but he was still standing before the sink with his back to us.

"He's dead," Dad said. "He was dead when he hit the ground."

Mr. Orloff sobbed once, his arms braced against the sink. Then he reached again into the locked cabinet and pulled out a box of hypodermics. Clear-eyed, he handed it to Auntie. "You will need to administer the remainder of the doses," he told her. "One shot every four hours until the wound stops seeping. If you run out of doses before that happens, then it was too late." His voice broke, and he rested a hand on the back of Rafe's head. "My beautiful boy."

"Why are you giving these to me?" Auntie asked, confused. "Where are you going to be?"

"I'm sorry," Ben Orloff whispered, and set his jaw. Then he crumpled to the floor.

"Shit," Dad said, letting go of me. Auntie gasped and dropped to her knees beside Rafe's father. Dad pried his lips open and sniffed. "Cyanide," he said in disgust. "Did anyone see him take it?"

We looked at one another, baffled. All of our attention had been on Rafe.

Perun faded in. "Coyote, We have a problem," He began. Then He spied Mr. Orloff's body on the floor. "Ah. I see you have the same problem."

Mom's eyes widened. "They all took cyanide?"

"All of them," Perun confirmed. "Even the worms. As well as the two half-worms behind the locked partition in the barn." He shook His head. "Such a waste."

"That means Rafe's the only survivor," I said, taking his hand. He was still unresponsive, but his chest rose and fell slightly. And I thought his color was a bit better, although that may have been wishful thinking.

"We'll have to contact someone," Auntie said, straightening.

"Don't worry, Sadie. We'll take care of it," Mom said. "You tend to your son." She looked at Perun. "Would You please get us out of here?"

He nodded. "Of course. But you will want to pick up Rafe first."

Dad crossed to the head of the exam table and slipped his arms under Rafe's shoulders. I grabbed his feet, and nodded to Perun. And in a blink, we were back in the community house.

"Thank the gods you're back," Webb said, as Dad and I eased Rafe onto a bench. His arms flopped to the floor, so I picked them up and crossed them over his chest.

"Why?" Mom asked. "What's going on?"

"Look outside," Hilary said, twisting her folded hands.

Mom gave her a puzzled glance as she and Dad stepped to the front door and stuck their heads out. Mom drew back in a hurry. "It's snowing."

"It's not just snowing," Dad said. "It's a blizzard out there. What happened, anyway?"

"That's what I'm trying to tell y'all," Hilary said, her face ashen. "Enkou pulled the plug."

Chapter 17

You know that whole forty days and forty nights thing in the Bible? That's how long it snowed.

It would have been even longer, but despite Hilary and Webb's best efforts, the World Tree's taproot did finally reach the catchment basin. They were sure all was lost. But while they were freaking out about it, Veles came by and basically yelled at them for holding up the process. As it turns out, the World Tree is a giant atmospheric recycling device. Any moisture sucked up by its roots gets put back into our atmosphere – but gradually. It doesn't cause a single ten-foot-deep snowfall across the Northern Hemisphere from the Arctic to the tropics.

Hilary was ready to kill Enkou, but Veles talked her down. And then He had a little talk with Enkou, one Trickster to another. I guess it didn't exactly have the effect Hilary was hoping for, because Enkou came away from the discussion munching on the biggest cucumber she'd ever seen.

That's what I heard, anyway. I couldn't get away to help with any of it. I was too busy helping Auntie take care of Rafe.

Everything shut down due to the unprecedented snowfall. We managed to get back to Anchorage before the roads became impassable, but in terms of getting back to Colorado by air or ground, we were all out of luck.

Mom started hyperventilating on about day three. She was hot to get home because Webb was supposed to take the ACT the following Saturday, but the test got postponed due to the snow. Then she was hot to get home because I was going to miss class, but CU canceled classes due to the snow. "Nobody's cooperating with me," she complained to Dad, who laughed at her.

On day four, she remembered that Grandfather was still living in his yurt, and then she was *really* hot to get home. At that point, she prevailed upon the gods, and White Buffalo Calf Pipe Woman agreed to do the honors. So Mom, Dad, Webb, and Hilary got ready to go. The goddess would have taken Hilary all the way to her parents' house, but she accepted Mom's invitation to stay with my parents in Golden. It was a lot closer to Boulder for when the campus reopened. "And anyway," she said, "have you ever been in North

Carolina when it snows? My father says a six-inch snowfall in Raleigh is when two flakes fall within six inches of each other." She shook her head. "I just can't imagine how they're coping with this."

Nawth C'lina. Cain't. I shook my head. "What about Enkou?" I asked.

"Enkou," she said with disgust, "can fend for himself."

The goddess laughed at that. Then She turned to me. "And you, Sage? Are you coming home?"

"I can't," I said. "Not 'til Rafe is better." There had been thirty syringes in the box Mr. Orloff had given to Auntie. We had used twenty of them by that point, and his condition hadn't changed. He was still comatose, his skin was the same dusky red, and his wound was still seeping that purple gore. On the other hand, he hadn't yet begun to morph into a giant worm. But I worried that the serum was only postponing the process without effecting a cure, and that once it was gone, Rafe would be lost.

White Buffalo Calf Pipe Woman put one glowing hand on the top of my head. "You are right, of course," She said. "Your place is here with him."

I glanced at Mom, who looked like she wanted to contradict the goddess. Dad saw it, too, and put his arm around her shoulders.

The goddess, meanwhile, was thinking. "I will talk to Brighid," She said at last. "Perhaps She has knowledge of a way to hasten his recovery."

Within the hour, my family and Hilary had departed, and Brighid had come.

I knew Her because she was Aunt Shannon's deity. Brighid was a Celtic goddess who ruled not only healing, but poetry and smithcraft. Her emerald green dress was covered with a knotwork design, and She wore Her hair braided to keep it out of Her way.

Obviously, She was here right now in Her capacity as a healer. As Auntie and I hovered nearby, She took one look at Rafe and *tsk*ed. "Your man is in a bad way, isn't he, Sage?"

"He is," I admitted, looking sideways at Auntie. "But he's not my man."

Brighid chuckled. "It's only an expression, My dear." But She winked at me, and I felt my face grow warm.

Auntie seemed to be taking the parade of gods through her home in stride – or else she was too distraught over Rafe's condition to hold any of Them in awe. "Can You help him?" she asked Brighid.

The goddess touched his forehead and frowned in surprise. She turned his head to examine the wound, and *tsk*ed again. "I may be able to, at that. Have you any tea?"

"Why, yes," Auntie said. "Several kinds. Do you think it will help him?"

"Well, it will help us," She said with a chuckle. "It's likely to be a bit of a wait."

Auntie smiled. "I'll go heat some water," she said, and left the room.

Brighid's smile faded. "I didn't want her to overhear this," She confided in me. "He's in a bad way, Sage. I can heal him, sure, but the cure may be worse than the disease."

I blinked. "Worse than letting him turn into a giant ice worm?"

"Is that what he's got?" She stared down at him. "In that case, no, I suppose not. But it's not going to be a day at the fair." She picked up one of the syringes in the box on the nightstand. "What's this supposed to be, then?" She asked, examining the contents.

"The antidote. His father said to give him a shot every four hours."

"Tch. It's junk. Throw it away." She dropped the syringe back in the box and shoved the whole thing at me. As I grabbed it reflexively, She bent down and murmured in Rafe's ear, "It's going to feel a little like I'm drawing your brain out of your skull now, and I'm sorry for it. But it must be done if you're to heal." Still crouched over him, She told me to shut the door and hand her the plastic bag we'd been using for the cloths soiled with the purple ooze – both of which I did. Then She blew out a breath as mighty as if Her lungs were a blacksmith's bellows, sealed Her mouth around the suppurating wound, and began to suck.

Periodically, She would straighten and spit a glob of gunk into the plastic bag. Sometimes, the gunk would seem to writhe, and at that point I had to look away.

After about ten minutes of this treatment, Rafe let out a moan – the first sound he had made since his collapse up north. "That's My boy," Brighid said encouragingly, and patted his shoulder. Then She went back to Her work.

A minute later, Auntie knocked. "The hot water's ready for tea," she said. "May I come in?"

Brighid straightened and wiped Her mouth with the back of Her hand. "Just one moment, Sadie. I've nearly – aha!" She plucked something out of the wound and held it up in triumph. "Gotcha, you little bugger! Come in, Sadie, and see what I've fetched out of your son's skull."

Auntie slowly opened the door and peered in. Her mouth dropped open when she saw the wriggling thing Brighid held between Her thumb and forefinger. "Is that the worm?" she asked, one hand going to her cheek.

"It is indeed," the goddess said, looking positively pleased with Herself. "Have you a closed container of some sort? A jar with a tight-fitting lid, perhaps?"

Auntie ran to check the recycling bin. Soon she was back with a pickle jar. "It's all I could find," she said.

"That will do nicely," said Brighid, and plopped the worm in the jar.

Auntie screwed the lid on tight. Then she said, "What should we do with it?"

"Hold it for now," said the goddess. "Perhaps Rafe will want to make a pet of it." At Auntie's confused look, She laughed in delight. "Don't look so stricken, Sadie! I was only joking. I'll take it to Manannan mac Lír. The sea is His domain, even the parts that are frozen all the time. He'll know what to do with it."

As this exchange went on, I looked over our patient. "He looks better, I think," I said now. The dusky pallor was fading. While his skin was far from its usual coffee color, he no longer looked like a purple tomato. And the fluid seeping from his wound was blessedly clear.

"He does," said Auntie in relief.

"And so would you, if your head had been relieved of this hairy thing," said Brighid with a laugh. "Let's have that tea."

After a cheerful half-hour in Auntie's living room, Brighid rose to look in on Rafe again. She gave us a pleased nod when she returned. "He's much improved," She said. "I expect he'll regain consciousness before the morning. Give him plain water at first, and if he tolerates that, then some broth or weak tea. I'll be back by in the morning."

"I don't know how to thank You," Auntie said.

"Tch. No thanks are due," the goddess said. She nodded at me. "Sage and her team have done yeoman's work these few days past. It's the least I could do to repay that." She scooped up the pickle jar. "See you tomorrow." And She faded out.

I let Auntie have some time alone with her son. Then I sent her off to bed for a few hours' rest, and took up my station in the rocking chair next to Rafe's bed.

He really did look better. The purple hue was nearly gone, and he had turned onto his side. I could see a bruise beginning to form around the edges of his wound, and couldn't help but snicker. Brighid had given him a hickey.

I'd nodded off over my tablet, but I came awake instantly when I heard Rafe call my name.

"Hey there," I said softly, and reached for his hand. "You're awake."

He squeezed my hand weakly, and my heart soared. "Yeah," he said. "I guess. How long have I been out of it?"

"Four days. No, five. How do you feel?"

"Like someone took a vacuum cleaner to my head," he said, putting his free hand to his forehead.

I laughed. "Someone did. Brighid. She's got lungs like you wouldn't believe."

"Brighid? Like, the goddess Brighid? How did I rate that?"

I grinned at him. "Family connections."

"I should have known."

"Want some water?"

"Yeah, that would be good." I helped him sit up and sat next to him on the bed as I guided a glass to his lips. We both laughed as he spilled a little. I put the glass down and brushed it off his t-shirt. He stilled my hand beneath his own.

His skin was still a little purple, but his eyes hadn't changed a bit – they were every bit as beautiful as I'd thought, the first time I saw them. I kissed him gently and sat back. "I'm so glad you're better," I said, and tears spilled down my cheeks.

"That bad?" he asked as I wiped my face with my sleeve.

"Yeah. That bad."

He was all seriousness now. "What did I miss?"

I put on a cheerful face. "We did it, Rafe. We defeated Vasily. And we got the water back." I told him about Enkou pulling the plug, and about the taproot of the World Tree, and about our endless snowstorm. "Classes are canceled for at least two weeks," I finished. "So don't worry. You have plenty of time to get well."

"What about my father?" he asked.

For a moment, I could only shake my head. "He didn't make it," I said at last.

Rafe nodded, as if he'd expected it.

"I'll get your mom," I said.

"No," he said. "Not yet." He lay back down, exhausted. "I think I'd like to go back to sleep for a little while."

"Okay." I started to slide off the bed, but he clutched my hand.

"Stay with me," he said, his voice already fading into sleep. "Don't leave me, Sage."

I stretched out next to him, on top of the covers. "Don't worry," I whispered. "I'm not going anywhere without you."

The last word...for now

You didn't really think I would let Sage have the final word, did you?

Oh, she spins a pretty good yarn. I'll give her that. And at least she's starting to treat me like an adult. But we have a long way to go before our tale is done.

If you want, I could tell you right now what's going to happen in the rest of the story. You know I already know the ending – it's on the final panel of the project in my room at home. It would save us all a lot of time in the long run.

But then, as my big sister has observed, nothing about the future is set in stone. Despite what I've already put in that final panel, things could still change.

And anyway, what makes you think that I would tell you the truth? I'm a Trickster, after all, just like my dad. And Sage would be the first to advise you not to believe anything I say.

Author's Note

I always knew those Curtis kids would lead me astray. Here I am, a fantasy writer, and yet Sage and Webb have forced me to delve into science fiction.

I wish I could say that I made up methane ice worms, but no, they are an actual thing. The kind that can make humans morph into giant slugs are wholly my own invention, though – and thank the gods for that, right?

As for hovercars, I'm with Naomi: I'm still waiting for my flying car, and I am not happy about the delay.

When it comes to climate change, though? I'm convinced both that it's real, and that humanity is changing our planet faster than would have happened otherwise. Besides a fair amount of research on the interwebs, I've relied on two books for my view of Sage and Webb's world, and of what Sage faces as she tries to heal the Earth: *Climate Change: What It Means for Us, Our Children, and Our Grandchildren*, edited by Joseph F.C. DiMento and Pamela Doughman; and *The World in 2050: Four Forces Shaping Civilization's Northern Future*, by Laurence C. Smith.

The Bear Mother myth comes from *Heroes & Heroines in Tlingit-Haida Legend* by Mary G. Beck. Another of Beck's books, *Potlatch*, was also a useful reference.

I owe my thanks to my editorial team, Susan Strayer and Kat Milyko, who have done their usual stellar job in keeping me from making too big an idiot of myself. By the way, if you liked Enkou, you can thank Kat and Susan for pestering me into putting a kappa in this series. If Enkou annoyed you, however – well, now you know who to blame.

If you're the sort of reader who doesn't like for a series to leave you hanging for too long, I have good news for you: Book 2, *Firebird's Snare*, is coming along nicely. I hope to release it next month, around the summer solstice. To get the first word on its release, please click here to sign up for my spam-free newsletter. I'll also post the info at my blog and on my Facebook page, but the newsletter is your guaranteed way to find out.

One more thing: If you enjoyed *Dragon's Web* – or even if you didn't – won't you please go back where you purchased the book to post a review? Reviews are a key way that readers find good books, and I treasure each and every review that my books receive. Thank you in advance!

Lynne Cantwell
May 2015

About the Author

Lynne Cantwell writes mostly urban fantasy and paranormal romance, with a dash of magic realism when she's feeling more serious. She is also a contributing author for Indies Unlimited. In a previous life, she was a broadcast journalist who worked at Mutual/NBC Radio News, CNN, and a bunch of other places you have probably never heard of. She has a master's degree in fiction writing from Johns Hopkins University. Currently, she lives near Washington, D.C.

Discover other Kindle titles by Lynne Cantwell:

The Maidens' War
SwanSong
Seasons of the Fool

The Pipe Woman Chronicles:
Seized
Fissured
Tapped
Gravid
Annealed
The Pipe Woman Chronicles Omnibus

Land, Sea, Sky:
Where Were You When: An Anthology
Crosswind
Undertow
Scorched Earth
The Land, Sea, Sky Trilogy

The Pipe Woman's Legacy:
Dragon's Web
Firebird's Snare (summer 2015)

Indies Unlimited 2012 Flash Fiction Anthology (contributor)
Indies Unlimited 2013 Flash Fiction Anthology (contributor)

Indies Unlimited Tutorials and Tools for Prospering in a Digital World (contributor)
Indies Unlimited Tutorials and Tools for Prospering in a Digital World, Vol. II (contributor)
BookGoodies How to Write A Book (contributor)
First Chapters (contributor)
13 Bites (contributor)
Summer Dreams (contributor)
Boo!: Volume 2 (contributor)
Winter Tales (contributor)
Plan 559 from Outer Space (contributor)

Find Lynne on Teh Intarwebz:

Facebook: http://www.facebook.com/pages/Lynne-Cantwell
Twitter: http://twitter.com/lynnecantwell
Google Plus: http://plus.google.com/+LynneCantwell
Goodreads:
http://www.goodreads.com/author/show/696603.Lynne_Cantwell
Blog: http://www.hearth-myth.com

Turn the page for a preview of
Firebird's Snare:
Book 2 of the Pipe Woman's Legacy

coming in the summer of 2015!

When Rafe and I got off the hypersonic plane at Denver International Airport, we thought we were going to go right back to our lives as if nothing had happened.

Boy, were we wrong.

I mean, sure, everything was still covered in snow. And when I say covered, I'm not kidding. You know that old photo that gets posted online every winter where the snow on either side of the road is taller than a tour bus? That's pretty much how everything looked everywhere – in Anchorage when Rafe's mom drove us to the airport from his house, on the tarmac in both Anchorage and Denver, and all the land we could see from the air. Mountains, valleys, towns – everything was buried under a massive blanket of white. It looked really pretty from the air.

Oh, come on. I'm not a total idiot. Alaska does have internet access, and I knew the tropics were having trouble digging out. I also knew people in temperate latitudes around the world were dying from the sudden cold. But it's one thing to see video on the news, and another thing entirely to have a couple of armed soldiers stop you as you step off the jetway. Especially when the whole thing wasn't really your fault.

"Sage Curtis?" one of the soldiers barked as he stepped into our path.

I stopped in surprise, and Rafe bumped into me from behind. Rafe had been doing pretty well at staying upright – especially given that he'd been comatose, with a disgusting iceworm stuck in his head, until just a few days before – but the travel had worn him out, and I think he just wanted to go home and go to bed.

"Yes?" I said. Then I stepped aside, realizing we were blocking the jetway exit and holding up the other passengers.

"Raphael Orloff?" the soldier went on, looking at Rafe.

"Present and accounted for," he said, with a sloppy salute.

I threw him a panicked look and turned to the nice man with the gun. "Please excuse him," I said in some haste. "He's had a rough couple of weeks."

Thank goodness the soldier didn't seem put out. All he said was, "Follow me, please," and turned on his heel to head out into the hallway between the gates. Rafe and I shrugged and fell into step behind him. The second soldier fell in behind us.

It was late, so the airport wasn't crowded. But still, our little procession drew some looks. "Um," I said, "we're not under arrest, are we?"

Neither of the soldiers responded.

Rafe looked at me sidelong and said in my head, *They didn't handcuff us.*

True enough, I replied the same way. We had discovered this mind-to-mind communication trick just a few weeks before, while he was teaching me how to fly. And when I say "fly," I mean fly like a bird flies – he's allied with Raven and I'm allied with Thunderbird. It's a long story why I was just learning now, at the ripe old age of nineteen.

So we could probably leave any time we wanted to, he went on.

I glanced back pointedly at the armed soldier behind us. *You want to try it?*

He shot me a mischievous grin. *I bet if we shifted, we could get away before they figured out what to do about it.*

I was just about to reply when the soldier in front of us stopped abruptly before an unmarked door. He knocked twice, opened the door without waiting for a response, and motioned us inside.

As soon as I saw who was waiting for us in the room beyond, I sent to Rafe, *No bet.* Then aloud, I said, "Captain Warren? What are you doing here?"

Captain Darrell Warren rose from the folding table he'd been sitting at and came toward us. "You can call me Darrell. I'm a civilian now." He shook hands with me, his grip firm. "Good to see you, Sage. And this must be Raphael."

"It's Rafe," he said, shaking hands in turn. Darrell slipped him a business card, and I watched Rafe's eyebrows shoot up as he read it.

"Like I said," I told him, with some satisfaction. Then I turned to Darrell. "He tried to bet me that your guys wouldn't be able to catch us if we shifted."

"Ah," Darrell said with a grin. "Nope, sorry. My unit has a fair amount of experience with that sort of thing."

Darrell was a friend of my parents. I'd met him in Washington, D.C., as my family joined forces with him and some of his friends to defeat Lucifer and keep the Earth humming along the way the gods wanted it. That was before Darrell had formed the quasi-military government agency he had been heading up since then. I didn't know a lot about it, but I knew it had something to do with keeping rogue gods – as well as rogue humans – from disturbing the peace the way Lucifer had. Darrell was perfect for the job. Not only was he a former Navy SEAL – and still built like one, I noted appreciatively – but he was also a Potawatomi Indian shaman who had a bit of shapeshifting ability himself.

Rafe was still looking at Darrell's business card. "What does JAF-H/D stand for?"

"Joint Assault Force Hominid/Deific," said a smug voice behind us. "I thought it up myself."

"Nanabush!" I cried, and crossed the room to give Him a hug. Darrell's god was dressed in buckskin, as usual. His eyes bugged out and His rabbity ears stood straight up in alarm when I put my arms around Him.

"Oh, relax, you old faker," said Darrell fondly. "And You did not think it up. I did."

"Well, I helped," He grumbled. Then his tone brightened. "Hi, Sage. You've grown since the last time I saw you."

"I would hope so," I said. "The last time You saw me, I was, what, fifteen?" I turned back to Darrell. "Do Mom and Dad know you're in town?" He and his wife, Tess Showalter, had come out to visit us a handful of times. Usually their friends Robbie and Sue Duckworth came then, too.

"No, and I'm afraid it's going to have to stay that way," Darrell told me. "This is an official visit."

"Clandestine," Nanabush said, hiding most of His face behind His generously fringed sleeve. "Cloak-and-dagger stuff. Need-to-know basis."

Darrell rolled his eyes and continued, "I wanted both of you to know that the government very much appreciates your actions on behalf of the Earth a few weeks back. I know it wasn't easy, and involved a measure of personal sacrifice. Especially for you, Rafe." Darrell laid a hand on Rafe's shoulder. "We'd been watching your father's operation for some time, but we didn't think it had reached a boil-over point. Obviously, we were wrong. I'm sorry."

"It's okay," Rafe said, but his eyes misted over. I glanced away to give him a moment of privacy.

I knew his feelings for his dad were complicated. Ben Orloff had been the one to implant the iceworm in his head. When we cornered him, he gave us a box of syringes loaded with a useless antidote, and then killed himself. Rafe would have been dead if the goddess Brighid hadn't been called in to heal him.

But still, Mr. Orloff had been Rafe's dad. And while he mourned the father he had loved, he also harbored a newfound hatred of the man. We'd talked about it in Anchorage, while Rafe was recovering from his brush with death. "I don't know, Sage," he had said. "I knew Dad was preoccupied with his job. He was one of those guys who was only present for a moment. You know? You'd ask him a question and his response would trail off partway through, and you just knew he had stopped thinking about what you'd asked him because he'd gone off on some unrelated tangent in his head."

I knew of at least one Environmental Engineering professor who had the same inability to have a conversation outside of his own head. Everybody avoided taking his classes. The material was notoriously difficult, and unless you got a decent teaching assistant for your section, you were pretty much going to be toast.

"But I always knew he loved me," Rafe said. Then he huffed a rueful laugh. "Or I thought I knew he did. Maybe I was wrong, all those years. Maybe he never loved me at all." He lay quietly for a moment. "I wonder whether he ever loved Paul."

"I'm sure he loved both of you," I said, although privately, I wondered. Paul and Rafe were born twenty years apart and had different mothers. Paul seemed to hate Rafe, and Rafe thought it was because his mother was Tlingit. But that was just conjecture on Rafe's part. If his mother knew the real reason, she wasn't telling.

I turned back to Darrell after a moment and said, "So you pulled us in here just to apologize? You didn't have to bring in an armed guard for that, you know. You could have just sent us an email or something."

Nanabush snickered, but Darrell barely cracked a smile. "Of course not. There's more." He moved back to the folding table. "Have a seat."

I slipped my fingers into Rafe's and squeezed. He blinked to clear his gaze and squeezed back. Then we sat down opposite Darrell.

He had put his hands flat on the table and was staring at them as if he didn't quite know how to begin. Then, abruptly, he cleared his throat and looked straight at us. "While the Earth is grateful to you both, your actions have created a problem."

I felt my face get hot. "The snow."

"The snow," he said, nodding. "Already, we're starting to see the effects of this massive world-wide weather event."

"I know people are dying," I began.

"Not just people, Sage. Livestock, too. And crops. The world's food supply is in jeopardy."

Nanabush popped in, perching on the edge of the table next to me. "You might say humanity will soon be in a world of hurt," He said with a wink.

"We're really sorry it happened," Rafe said. "But it's not our fault."

"It's Webb's," I said darkly, voicing the accusation that had been simmering in my head throughout Rafe's convalescence. "He and Hilary were supposed to keep an eye on Enkou, and they didn't."

"I'm not here to assign blame, Sage," said Darrell. "What's done is done. I'm not going to hold anybody responsible for the kappa's actions. He's a Trickster, and I know from first-hand experience that Tricksters do whatever they want." He threw the god a disgusted gaze, and Nanabush threw back his head and laughed in delight.

"So then what's this all about?" Rafe asked as Nanabush trailed off in giggles.

"We need to work toward mitigating the damage," Darrell said. "Near the equator, the world is already starting to warm up again. The snow will melt relatively quickly, and the total impact on life there should be minimal. But the runoff...."

"Is going to raise the sea level," Rafe said, sitting back in sudden understanding. "At least in the short term. It'll cause massive flooding all over the world."

"But in arid climates, won't the snow mostly evaporate?" I asked, thinking furiously. "Wait. That will overload the atmosphere with water vapor. It will make climate change way worse. Oh, my gods." I turned to Rafe. "We've got to *do* something. And we haven't got much time."

"There might be a way," Darrell said, and we turned to him as one. "While you were recovering, Rafe, Dr. Raymond from CU contacted me. It was actually his idea to bring you two on board."

"Why us?" I said. "It's not like we covered ourselves in glory the last time."

"I believe he said you know the players."

Rafe and I traded a look of dismay. "Oh, no," I said. "I am *not* going back down to Nav."

"Even to save the Earth?" Nanabush asked.

I gave Him a hard look. "That's not fair."

He shrugged. "Nobody ever said life was fair. Not even the gods."

I closed my eyes and sighed. Then I looked at Rafe, who was leaning on the table with his head down and his shoulders slumped. "Look," I said to Darrell, "it's late. I'm really tired from the trip, and he's" – I hooked a thumb at Rafe – "just about to fall over. Can we sleep on it?"

Darrell sat back. "Of course. But don't take too long to decide. You said it yourself – we don't have much time." He stood, and Nanabush shot off the table and stood at attention next to him. Then He winked at me, which made me smile.

"When do you graduate?" Darrell asked me as Rafe and I got to our feet.

The question caught me off-guard. "Not for another two-and-a-half years. But then I'll have a master's. Why?"

He ignored my question. "Rafe, how about you?"

He nodded tiredly. "Same-same."

"Well. If you two can pull this off, I can guarantee you both a job with my agency after graduation." Before I could respond, he handed me one of his cards. "This number is a secure line. I always answer it. If you have any questions, don't hesitate to give me a call."

"All right," I said.

"Oh," Darrell said, fishing in his pocket. "There was one other thing I was supposed to tell you." He extracted a different business card – this one prominently featuring the NWNN logo – and handed it to me. "Tess wants to talk to you."

I looked up at him in surprise. "Why?"

"She wants to interview you, of course," Nanabush said brightly. "You two are national heroes!"

www.ingramcontent.com/pod-product-compliance
Lightning Source LLC
Chambersburg PA
CBHW071254130626
46556CB00003B/1309